D0113987

30,614

M

Landrum Landrum, Graham

The historical
society murder
mystery

THE
HISTORICAL
SOCIETY
MURDER MYSTERY

ALSO BY GRAHAM LANDRUM

The Sensational Music Club Mystery
The Rotary Club Murder Mystery
The Famous DAR Murder Mystery

THE
HISTORICAL
SOCIETY
MURDER MYSTERY

Graham Landrum

AS REPORTED BY
HELEN DELAPORTE,
HARRIET GARDNER BUSHROW,
AND THEIR FRIENDS

ST. MARTIN'S PRESS
NEW YORK

A THOMAS DUNNE BOOK.
An imprint of St. Martin's Press.

All characters and events in *The Historical Society Murder Mystery* are entirely imaginary, with no basis in fact whatsoever.

Library of Congress Cataloging-in-Publication Data

Landrum, Graham.
    The historical society murder mystery   /   by Graham Landrum.
        p.   cm.
    "A Thomas Dunne book."
    ISBN 0-312-14355-9
    I. Title.
PS3562.A4775H57   1996   95-53354
813'.54—dc20   CIP

First Edition: June 1996

10 9 8 7 6 5 4 3 2 1

THE
HISTORICAL
SOCIETY
MURDER MYSTERY

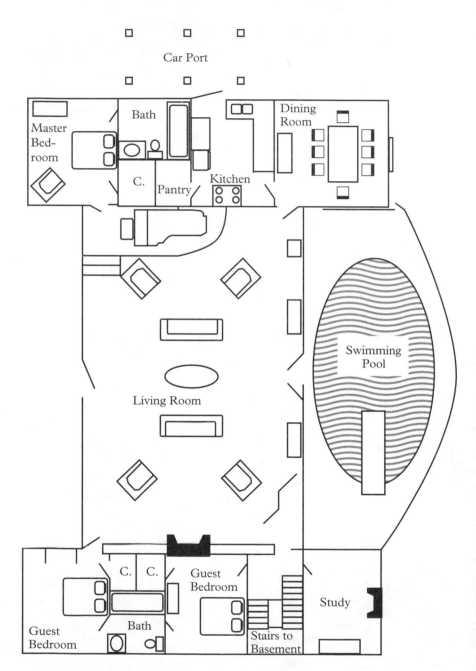

Floor Plan of the Ground Floor of Randy Hartwell's House

Alberta Chamberlain's Death

HELEN DELAPORTE

"Alberta Chamberlain died."

"Yes?"

"She has been sick such a terribly long time!"

Henry made no answer. He was deep in the letters-to-the-editor—that other portion of the *Borderville Banner-Democrat* that must by all means be read: "who's dropping off" and "who's popping off" being of equal interest in our little city.

The obituary read:

> Alberta Brockton Chamberlain of 902 Chestnut Street died yesterday in Borderville Memorial Hospital after a lengthy illness. A leader of local society, Mrs. Chamberlain was born in Philadelphia, coming here in 1925 as the bride of the late Nathan Chamberlain, who for many years was involved regionally in the lumber business. Mrs. Chamberlain held degrees from Bryn Mawr College and the Drexel Institute. She leaves no close relatives. Arrangements are pending.

"She's been in the hospital so long, poor dear!"

As Henry offered no comment, I went on.

"They really should have given her a better write-up. . . . Henry, are you listening?"

Henry put down his section of the paper and said, "Something about Mrs. Chamberlain?"

"I was saying that the *Banner-Democrat* should have given more details in her obituary. After all, there was a time not so long ago when she was very important in this town. But she's been out of circulation for a while, and now it's as though she could have been just anybody at all."

I remembered her air of self-assurance and the way people deferred to her. Not just because she was rich—it was more than that. She was a very intelligent woman, very capable, always working in charity drives—active in the beautification program and a pillar of the Presbyterian Church. She was a great bird watcher and promoter of the Appalachian Trail. But there are so many young people at the *Banner-Democrat* now, and they would not remember any of that.

"Henry!"

"Yes?"

"Do you remember that years ago she promised to leave her portrait of Louis-Philippe to the Historical Society?"

"No." Henry had his nose in the editorial page again.

"Henry!"

He looked up, and this time I knew that I had his attention.

"Mrs. Chamberlain had an ancestor in Philadelphia, a wealthy merchant—way back—who commissioned Charles Willson Peale to paint a portrait of Louis-Philippe—the one, you remember, who later became King of France. The picture came through her family eventually to her, and it hangs on the landing of her stairs. You have seen it—yes, you have!"

Henry was wearing that blank look he always wears when he doesn't know what I am talking about.

I went on: "It's full-length—with a rural background. Louis has a straw hat in his hand. You couldn't possibly forget it."

A hint of recollection came into Henry's eyes.

"I suppose so," he said. "Now why are you so excited about this portrait?"

"Well," I said, "she promised to leave it to the Historical Society."

" 'Promised to leave' and 'left' are two different things," Henry said, "and if she actually left it to the Society, what are you planning to do with it?"

The sarcastic tone in which Henry chose to express his question was undoubtedly brought on by the clutter of seven cardboard boxes in our guest bedroom—boxes of papers, letters, a family Bible or two. The Society had received them last June, and now, the following April, I had still not decided just what should be done with them.

"I'll get somebody else to take care of the portrait," I promised.

I should explain that although I am not a native of this area and live on the Tennessee side of Borderville, I am a member of the Ambrose County Historical Society, Ambrose County being in Virginia; and last spring I was elected president of the organization.

I was greatly flattered, because people around here are suspicious of incomers. Our folk are very warm-hearted, but so much has been said about Appalachia by outsiders, and so much of it has dealt with our poverty, ignorance, and squalor—all of which is to be found here but isn't an accurate picture—so much has been said that people in this region who are not squalid, ignorant, or poor brace themselves when they see a Yankee coming. Will the newcomer bring with him a kind of missionary, condescending sympathy for our benighted lot? Or will he—or often she—meet us on our own terms? There is a kind of face-off, you see, when the newcomer meets Appalachia in all its variety.

People here have a strong feeling of *us* and *them*. It has taken me a quarter of a century to move into the charmed circle. And when I was elected president of the Ambrose County (Virginia) Historical Society in spite of the fact that I am a Yankee and live on the Tennessee side of the state line, I realized that I had indeed come through all the progressive stages of acceptance—from my job as organist at Saint Luke's, to the Wednesday Study Club, to the board of the YWCA, to the presidency of the Borderville Music Club, to the regency of the Old Orchard Fort Chapter, NSDAR, and at last to the presidency of the Ambrose County Historical Society. There can never be any doubt that now I am not one of *them,* but one of *us.*

Under these circumstances, naturally, I was determined that my two years of office should be not merely a success but also evidence of my loyalty to and affection for these dear and wonderful people.

But to get back to the portrait of Louis-Philippe.

Mrs. Chamberlain had said rather frequently that the only occasion when it had been on public display was at the Philadelphia Exposition of 1876.

There is actually a minor connection between our area and Louis-Philippe, who lived in Philadelphia between 1796 and 1800, and became the "Citizen King of France" in 1830. Difficult as it is to believe, in 1796 Louis traveled through the Valley of Virginia into Tennessee in order to look at Indians. In the process he spent the night of April 24 through 25 at Ambrose Courthouse. And what is even more amazing, he wrote about it in his journal.

Mrs. Roosevelt came through here many times, and Lady Bird Johnson was here once; but so far as I know, Louis's visit is the only brush with royalty it has been our privilege to enjoy.

Faint though our claim to Louis is, I found it exciting that our Society was to receive his portrait, particularly since it was painted by Charles Willson Peale, who produced so many portraits of Washington and other founding fathers.

Of course it was difficult to know exactly what to do with such a large painting, but perhaps we could hang it in the courtroom at Ambrose Courthouse. And wouldn't it be a spiffy attraction during the festival in August! The Chamber of Commerce would surely be pleased about that.

For the present, however, the main thing was to take possession of the canvas—and of course Henry was right: we couldn't have the thing in our house, leaning against the wall for months while we considered where to give it a proper home.

As Henry left for the office, I said, "Now, you are going to find out about the will and see if Mrs. Chamberlain really did leave the picture to us?"

"Of course," he said.

Henry pretends to look on many of my activities with a jaundiced eye, but he is very tolerant of them; in fact, he is proud of the offices I have held and has often admitted that my little community efforts have been advantageous to his law practice. I knew Henry would bring me the information as soon as possible.

And sure enough, only two days later he reported the

Chamberlain will had been drawn by Angus Redloch—that dear old man, now dead, who helped with the DAR mystery.* The will was in the hands of Gilmer Nichols, and Henry had seen it and affirmed that Mrs. Chamberlain had duly and faithfully left "the full-length portrait of Louis-Philippe, the French King, painted by Charles Willson Peale" to the Ambrose County Historical Society as she had promised. Kevin Summerthwait was designated the administrator, and Henry advised me to see him as soon as the will had been proved and Kevin had his letters testamentary.

Henry need not have urged me to promptness. I remembered only too well that after my mother's death in Swarthmore, the house was burglarized and we lost a number of valuable items.

I don't like to say how many years it has been since I took Art History 101, but I remembered a few things about Charles Willson Peale, such as that he had several sons, all named for famous artists. Now that our Society was to receive a painting by so noted a hand, I thought I should refresh my recollection with a quick look at the *Encyclopaedia Britannica*. This is what I found:

Charles Willson Peale was born in Maryland in 1741. He studied art with Copley and West. He was an officer in the American Revolution and was a prolific portraitist of figures important in the early years of our republic. He was a friend of Benjamin Franklin; and like Franklin, he had a consuming interest in science, which led to the creation of a museum of natural history in Philadelphia.

It seems that Peale and all his family made a business of producing portraits of Washington, etc., which, no doubt, would decrease the going price of a "Washington" painted by a Peale, but I hoped that the rarity of a "Louis-Philippe" by Peale would raise the importance of our canvas.

I was excited about this thing. I thought I might insert something about it in the next *Alumnae Bulletin*. Perhaps something like this: Helen (Dudley) Delaporte, class of '52, reports that the Ambrose County (Va.) Historical Society, of which she is president, has received the bequest of a portrait of Louis-Philippe, King of France 1830–48, painted by Charles Willson Peale.

If I had only known how much trouble that dratted portrait would cause!

In fact, I did one sensible thing immediately. I called Bob Kelsey, secretary of the Society. He is a very efficient gentleman, just retired from the postal service and willing to do anything for the Society at my merest suggestion. He is native-born—that is to say, Appalachian—quite intelligent, and an avid amateur of local history. Besides, he has a van.

So I called him and asked him to secure the portrait for us and keep it, if it wasn't "too much trouble," until we could arrange a permanent place to display it. I gave him Kevin Summerthwait's number and explained that I would speak to Kevin about the matter. Then, after I had made the arrangements with Kevin, I left the whole thing to the two of them and felt that the acquisition of our painting was a fait accompli.

In about a week Bob called and said that he had the canvas. Where? Leaning up against the wall in his guest bedroom.

How could we live without guest bedrooms?

I was pleased with the way things had progressed. In the meantime the April meeting had already passed. It would have been perfect if we could have had the canvas there. But even without it, a great deal of excitement was generated among the members. I appointed a committee to consider what we should do with our portrait of Louis. Once more, as happened every two or three years, it was the opinion of all of us that Ambrose County really ought to have a historical museum. The examples of Tazewell, with its museum and reconstruction of Witten's Fort, and Burke County, with the restoration of Soldier's Retreat, were brought up. But we all knew it would take fifty years to raise enough funds for such a project. The courthouse seemed to be the only viable repository for our most recent acquisition.

Without my prior knowledge, Bob gave a press release to the *Ambrose County Weekly*. I was therefore surprised a few days later to read the following in that very interesting publication:

RARE PORTRAIT GIVEN TO HISTORICAL SOCIETY

Receipt of a full-length portrait of Louis-Philippe, King of France, was reported at the April meeting of the Ambrose County Historical Society by Bob Kelsey, secretary of the organization. The full-length portrait, measuring 68 by 36 inches, had been in the family of the late Mrs. Nathan Chamberlain since it was painted in Philadelphia in the 1700s. It was last on public display in 1876 at the Philadelphia Centennial Exhibition.

The portrait artist was Charles Willson Peale, noted for his delineation of Washington and other notables of the federal period.

When or where this painting will be on public view has not been determined. "Plans are being discussed at the present time," Kelsey stated. "A public announcement will be made as soon as a suitable place for permanent display can be arranged."

And that is where the saga of Louis-Philippe's portrait stood the last week in April.

Then I read in the *Banner-Democrat* that the Herbert P. and Margaret M. Bennett Memorial Lecture at the college during the first week in May would be presented by Sterling Brenthauser, professor of art history at James River State University.

I called our college immediately, explained that I had known the professor's wife, Genevieve, for a number of years through the DAR, and asked if he/they could stay with us while in town. I was told that the Brenthausers would be guests of the president of the college, who did not offer to release them to my hospitality.

I asked the president's secretary if there was a time when I might be able to see these honored guests. "Yes," she said, after examining their schedule. "On Thursday afternoon, May 3, at three-fifteen, they will be arriving at Three City Airport. If you would care to meet them and bring them to the president's home, you could visit with them on the way to town."

On the way to town, indeed! But "on the way" can mean almost anything. I would simply plot that route so that it would go by the residence of Bob Kelsey, where there would be a pause and I would show our portrait of Louis-Philippe to an expert. I did not see why the Historical Society should keep its light under a bushel.

I sat down immediately and got off a note to Genevieve explaining our good fortune and our eagerness for Sterling to examine the canvas and advise us on cleaning, repair, and so forth.

Three days later I received a call from Genevieve expressing eagerness to see me. Sterling, she reported, was greatly interested in the painting because none of the studies of Peale's work to which he had access made mention of the Louis-Philippe portrait. She said Sterling was quite enthusiastic about the find.

May 3 came. When I picked up Genevieve and Sterling at the airport and announced that we would take a look at the portrait on the way to the campus, Sterling was delighted.

"You know," he said in his mild voice, "I have been trying to find out something about that painting ever since we received your letter. Though it is not in the catalog of Peale's works, it is obvious, when we consider how remarkably productive Peale was, that somewhere in the world there are others of his paintings. I am very eager to see the canvas. If it is one of his better works, it should be an excellent subject for a monograph. I believe you said there is some historical evidence for Louis's visit to this area?"

I had the details of that visit well in hand and recounted them in a matter of three minutes.

"That, of course, adds interest," Sterling observed. "Your historical group is very fortunate to receive such a distinguished picture. While I am sure that many portraits of Louis were painted in his later years, I doubt that many 'young' portraits on so large a scale survived the French Revolution."

You can imagine that talk of this sort had no dampening effect on my enthusiasm. I longed to ask Sterling just what price it might fetch if put up for sale, though I am sure we would never contemplate offering it. On the other hand, one never knows.

"You think, then, that it is a really valuable painting?" I finally asked.

"Certainly," he answered. "Any museum in the country would welcome the opportunity to acquire a Peale of such an unusual subject."

By the time I had stopped in front of the Kelseys' house, I was floating on a lovely pink cloud—all of this was so wonderful, and it was happening while I was president of the Society! Although I had done nothing to make it happen, the situation was very flattering to my ego.

Bob and Leota (Bob's wife) were expecting us—not in their Sunday best at all, but dressed more formally than retired people normally dress on a beautiful spring afternoon. They ushered us into their guest bedroom, where the painting, wrapped in an old sheet, was leaning against a wall.

Bob removed the covering, and there was our picture in its heavy, ornate frame.

"Oh," I exclaimed, "some of the gesso is missing." That's the gilt material with which picture frames were ornately decorated in Peale's day.

"I know," Bob explained. "It was that way when Mr. Summerthwait and I took it off the wall."

For some seconds Bob and I were occupied with the problem of the missing gesso—where could we get the frame repaired? how much would it cost? that kind of thing. As a result of this rather ridiculous concern, we were not immediately aware of the scrutiny Sterling was giving the portrait. We noticed, however, that something unusual was going on when he put his nose to the canvas and seemed to be smelling it.

He tilted the portrait away from the wall. The back of the painting was covered with what appeared to be oilcloth. There was a small tear in it where some minor accident had happened. The tacks with which the oilcloth was fastened to the back of the frame were rusty.

"Do you suppose we could remove this material?" Sterling asked.

I said, "Certainly."

Bob produced a pocket knife and began to pry out the tacks, revealing. . . .

Well, it was a shock. The canvas on which our Peale portrait was painted was brand new!

"And you say this painting is supposed to have hung in a house here in Borderville for some years?" Sterling asked.

With the evidence displayed before my eyes, it was obvious that this canvas was not the one that had hung in Mrs. Chamberlain's house when I had last been there—perhaps as much as ten years before.

"I don't understand," I said. "I'm certain that a portrait of Louis-Philippe has hung in Mrs. Chamberlain's house for at least thirty years. Just look at the frame. And this stuff tacked to the back of it. It all looks so old—and yet—?"

"It would seem," Sterling said, "that your organization has been cheated out of a valuable painting. The substitution is quite recent—within a matter of a month or so. We can take it without question that the frame is that of the original portrait. The backing itself, which concealed the freshness of the canvas, is also old. But between the frame and the backing someone has substituted a copy—quite a recent one, because it still has the odor of the medium or, if you prefer, the oil that bonds the pigment to the canvas."

Had I been in condition to do so, I might have replied to this lecture. As it was, I was speechless.

"You say this picture was received by bequest?"

I nodded.

Sterling continued, "From the estate of an older person?"

"Yes," I said.

"And it was in this person's house—not stored or anything of that sort—until how recently?"

"Just under two weeks ago," Bob offered.

"Was the person in the home without interval until the time of death?"

"No," I explained. "Mrs. Chamberlain was in the hospital for several months before she died."

"Then it seems that someone entered the house, copied the original—and left the copy in lieu of the genuine painting."

But that made no sense to me at all. "Why substitute a copy," I asked, "when all the thief had to do was steal the picture and vanish?"

"Dear lady," Sterling said, "I am only an art historian. My wife, however, informs me that *you* are the detective." He was referring, of course, to my part in the solution of the DAR case.

There seemed nothing further to be done just then about our spurious portrait of Louis. I was bound in duty to deliver Genevieve and Sterling to Dr. Markham's house. And then I would have to get Henry's dinner before I returned to the campus for Sterling's lecture at eight o'clock.

Throughout the lecture my mind was occupied by the afternoon's disclosure. Why, why, why? It would have been so much simpler to steal our painting without doing us the invidious favor of substituting a copy, the production of which must have entailed great effort, craft, and danger of detection. So, why? No answer came. I cannot have heard more than two words that Sterling said in his no doubt interesting lecture. I found it very awkward to speak to him afterward. Do you say "Thanks!" to a man for telling you your painting is a forgery?

The next morning I said to Henry, "What do you know about Kevin Summerthwait?"

"The executor of the Chamberlain will—he's a Kiwanian. I don't know anything else against him. Why?" (Henry is a Rotarian and was trying to be funny.)

"Tell me about him," I demanded.

"If you want to know if he stole your painting," Henry said, "the answer is no. Kevin is in the roofing business. He is as honest as the next man. And you can rest assured that if he were going to steal anything, it would never be a painting."

That was the end of that theory. I tried something else.

"As administrator of the Chamberlain estate, would Kevin be liable for the value of the picture?"

"If you could show that the loss resulted from his negligence. But please note: you and your friend Kelsey secured the painting—fake that it is—perhaps two days, three days, possibly four, after Kevin became administrator. How could he have found an artist to make the copy in that length of time? That means that the actual theft took place before he became administrator; in fact, before Mrs. Chamberlain's death.

"On the other hand," Henry continued, "you must notify Kevin. He should be alerted in order to discover whatever else may have been stolen. He also needs to know that someone has a key or other means of entry to the Chamberlain house—presuming of course that there are no signs of anyone's breaking in.

"Certainly at that level Kevin has an interest in the matter. And then, of course, if the genuine painting can be found, it would still be a part of the estate, and it would belong to your Historical Society. In any event there may be insurance, though it is by no means clear that your organization would be entitled to the proceeds."

Henry is the perfect husband. He lets me go my way, and when things become tangled, as they had in this case, he has the advice that is never wrong.

And I needed advice.

"So, what must I do?"

"Well," Henry began, "I suppose the first thing would be for Kevin to report the theft to the police." He paused a moment, weighing the situation. "Of course they won't know what to do about it," he acknowledged. "I don't suppose there has ever been an art theft in Borderville before this."

Henry was right. I could almost see the blank stare on Police Detective Cochran's face upon being confronted with this problem. It wasn't at all like recovering TV sets, rifles, PCs, and radial tires. But at least the theft should be investigated.

"I don't know how stolen art is marketed, but I should think," Henry continued, "that a picture of some age, painted by a known artist, will not be sold at a flea market. If I am right about it, the best price would be obtained through an auction house—no doubt one that specializes in artworks.

"Of course I have no idea what precautions those houses take to assure themselves of the legal ownership of the items they handle, but I should think that a thief who could manage to substitute a copy for the original could also forge documents of ownership."

Henry paused. Suddenly his eyes widened. "Oho!" he said. "That explains the need for the forged painting. The thief expects your organization to accept the substitution. Being local bumpkins, you will never know the difference. You'll be so thrilled with a royal portrait—one that will raise the tone of your historical collection and bestow an added glow of elegance upon your little southwestern Virginia city—you'll be so thrilled that you will hang the thing—I believe you were thinking of the courthouse?—where nobody of any expertise will see it. Schoolchildren will troop in to gaze upon it. I don't know how your DAR will like it that at last we have a king, but the citizens of Ambrose County will be happy. The portrait, fake though it is, will be a star in the crown of the historic little burg of Ambrose Courthouse. The forgery will serve all the purposes of the real thing.

"Meanwhile, our ingenious thief gets away with the real portrait, sells it at auction for, say, one hundred thousand dollars—I have no idea how much such a painting would bring. Then if he hasn't done the forgery himself, he pays the forger one thousand and has a profit of ninety-nine thousand. Not a bad caper!"

"Henry," I said, "you've hit the jackpot! How did you ever get to be so smart?"

"Well," he said, "I married this woman who keeps presenting me with problems, and I guess practice makes perfect."

That's my Henry, and I adore the man.

"I'm going to get a piece of paper and a pencil, and you're going to tell me exactly what to do," I said.

And that's what I did, and that's what he did. And here are the things I jotted down:

1. Contact Kevin Summerthwait. Have him look into the insurance angle. The company will have investigators who no doubt will aid in the search for the stolen property.

2. Notify police. Urge them to contact the Tennessee Department of Investigation if the local police don't know how to trace art theft. (Alberta lived on the Tennessee side of town.)

3. Do some library research. What are the important auction centers? Notify them.

4. Get an estimate of the value of the picture from Sterling Brenthauser.

5. Give the story to the *Banner-Democrat* and state that a reward will be presented to anyone providing information leading to the recovery, etc. (This last item, Henry explained, was to alert and interest the general public.)

All of these things, I did—with little success except for two items. First, when numbers 1 through 3 failed to produce results, we concluded that our stolen painting was still in Borderville hidden away somewhere, safely protected we hoped. Second, the story in the *Banner-Democrat* turned out to be important, as I shall now explain.

As soon as Henry had suggested the news story, I called the home of Dr. Markham, the president of the college. By luck, the Brenthausers were on the verge of leaving for the airport.

"Sterling," I said, getting immediately to the point, "I won't make you late. But just off the top of your head, estimate the value of the painting that was stolen."

"Oh . . ." He paused a moment. "If it is genuine and a good example of Peale's work and in good condition, I should think it would be worth perhaps something above a million."

I gasped. "Do you mean it?"

"Yes, I think that is a reasonable guess."

I thanked him, told him to have a good flight, and immediately called the paper.

The next morning we were greeted with the headline: MILLION-DOLLAR PAINTING STOLEN. We didn't know it then, but that headline would put in motion the events that eventually led us to the recovery of Louis's portrait. Of course the police responded to our complaint of the loss of our painting. They went out to Bob Kelsey's house, dusted the frame and back of the picture for fingerprints. They found Bob's prints and Kevin Summerthwait's (who had helped Bob fetch the picture from Alberta's house), mine, and Sterling Brenthauser's.

They also dusted for fingerprints at Alberta's house, but the thieves had apparently worn gloves when they took the picture from its place on the wall of the landing at the turning of that magnificent staircase.

The police questioned Mary Dugan, the Chamberlain housekeeper. They did everything I could have asked them to do. I had no reason to be dissatisfied with their investigation.

And I had done everything that could be expected of me; no one could have blamed me if I had resigned myself to do no more. Nevertheless, the loss of a million-dollar painting is nothing to be philosophical about. We had lost something of great value. I simply had to pursue the matter as far as I possibly could.

I had a faint memory of Mary Dugan, the Chamberlain housekeeper. She had been in evidence at the silver teas Mrs. Chamberlain used to put on for charity. That was back in the days when we still had silver coins and those coins would buy something. Every lady was expected to leave fifty cents in a tray on the table by the front door. Of course, many left much more, and Mrs. Chamberlain's affairs were always elegant. On those occasions, Mrs. Dugan—modestly but neatly dressed—unobtrusively renewed the goodies on the polished mahogany dining table. I decided to visit her and see whether I could elicit from her anything the police had not learned.

She was in the phone book as Mary Dugan and said she would be happy to see me.

Seated in her tiny living room crowded with bric-a-brac, we began our conversation by speaking of Mrs. Chamberlain. The poor woman had been housebound with arthritis—rarely so much as coming downstairs for many years. Still, she had been very insistent that everything in the house be kept as though guests would arrive at any instant.

"I am sure you knew every dish and vase in that house," I said.

"I did, indeed!" Mary replied. "I kept house for Mrs. Chamberlain for almost forty years. It was a big house but just a pleasure to work with all her beautiful things."

"Other than the painting, do you know of anything that may have been taken?" I asked.

"No, ma'am." The tone was certain. I believed what she said.

"Did you ever stay in the house and have a room there?" I went on.

"No. I have always lived here in my own home. I would get up at six every morning and get to Mrs. Chamberlain's in time to fix her breakfast. Then I would do the housework and the little bit of cooking that she wanted. There was nothing to the cooking—she ate so little. I just had to coax her. Then she got so that she had to have a nurse stay in the house with her around the clock five days a week, and another lady to come in on weekends.

"I would have liked to help Mrs. Chamberlain more, but with that big house, I couldn't nurse and do everything. All the time I was with Mrs. Chamberlain, she wasn't the only one that was getting older, you know."

"With you and two nurses," I asked, "how many keys to the house were there?"

"I had my key," she replied, "and the one nurse used Mrs. Chamberlain's key. I had to have a key made for the other nurse."

"I don't suppose an extra key could have been made at the shop where you had the key duplicated?"

"No. I stood right there while the girl made that other key."

"Was there evidence at any time that some outside person had gotten into the house?"

"Not at all. And I would swear that that picture never left the house until it was took down by those two men that come after Mrs. Chamberlain died."

I gathered that she meant Bob and Kevin.

"Of course, I never did what you might call check on it," she added, "but I would have known mighty quick if it wasn't on that wall. And I went into that house every day while Mrs. Chamberlain was in the hospital—just like she was paying me to do."

"And when Mrs. Chamberlain went to the hospital and the nurses didn't come anymore, what happened to the keys?"

"I took 'em."

The keys seemed to be accounted for, but the mystery was as murky as ever. If the picture never left the house, the copy must have been painted there. But that could hardly have happened since there had been no obvious break-in.

Still, there was a space of time between Mrs. Chamberlain's death and Kevin Summerthwait and Bob's arranging to pick up the picture. Where were the keys then? Could the forgery have been produced in the house at that time? Or perhaps the picture had been briefly removed from the house to be copied.

I put all these possibilities to Mary Dugan, but until Summerthwait received his letters testamentary, Mrs. Dugan had entered the house every day to water the plants, feed the cat, and take care of the mail. The cat had now been taken to the Humane Society, and Mary Dugan assured me that she had turned over all keys to Kevin Summerthwait as administrator. There had been no sign that an illicit entry to the house was made at any time.

What became of Alberta's plants? I didn't ask, but I noticed three vigorously blooming African violets in one window of Mary Dugan's sitting room and a luxuriant fern in the other. And certainly Mary Dugan deserved them.

As the result of my visit, I was no wiser than I had been before. I seemed to have proved that what I knew had happened hadn't happened at all. And yet Bob Kelsey had collected the picture at the earliest possible moment. It was frustrating, but Henry had been right about the thing that mattered most to me: the painting had been stolen through no fault of mine or of Bob Kelsey's. Nevertheless, I felt chagrin at the whole episode.

On the way home I detoured down Chestnut Street. Number 902, the Chamberlain house, stands on the corner in an area of huge old places built between 1910 and 1930. The street is lined with maples, which, I observed, would pretty well shield number 902 from the streetlight on the opposite corner.

I explored the side street. The blocks are shorter in that direction, and the Chamberlain house is divided from the nearest neighbor behind it by an alley. The lot across the alley, originally intended for one dwelling, had been divided, and two neat brick bungalows occupied the space. I knew who lived in one of them, the one next to the alley: Mrs. Paul Copeland, a widow, a member of Saint Luke's—

a dear little woman and deaf as a post. When she removed her hearing aid upon going to bed, no sound of any sort could possibly disturb her.

Nor could she have seen anything from her bedroom window because of the hedge—allowed to grow thick, no doubt to shield her from the alley.

There would be no difficulty in driving a car, lights out, into the alley any dark night, parking it there, and entering the Chamberlain property. I could see far enough up the alley to know that fences, trees, garages, and so on would obstruct the view from any direction and perhaps muffle any sound the intruder might make, such as the click of a door opening and closing or the sound of a motor being started.

The modus operandi of our art thief, then, would seem to have been something like this: after Mrs. Chamberlain was taken to the hospital and the nurses who had been with her at the house were discharged, late some night—probably well past midnight—he/she drove into that alley, entered the house, and did whatever he/she did to copy the picture.

But how?

Surely the process of painting so large a canvas and making the copy so exactly like the original that the substitution would go unnoticed by the untrained eye would take days, even weeks. The thief could hardly have done all that inside the Chamberlain house, because Mrs. Dugan returned to the house every day to feed the cat and give an eye to things in general.

I am a church organist and know nothing about painting, but I have been in artists' studios, and the smell of the oil and turpentine is quite strong. If Sterling Brenthauser could detect the odor several weeks after the painting was finished, surely Mary Dugan would have known by the smell that something very strange was going on if the portrait was actually copied in the Chamberlain house.

That would suggest that the forgery was painted somewhere else and brought into the house after it had been finished a few days. Besides, the forger would not have had room for his canvas, easel, and other paraphernalia on the landing. No, the work of copying had to have been done somewhere else.

Nor could it have been done by night in another room of the house and the original portrait replaced on the landing each time after the artist worked on the forgery. Activity of that sort, night after night, in any room would undoubtedly leave obvious traces of odor and paint that Mary Dugan would detect immediately. Light would be necessary for such work, and that would mean that special lamps would have to be brought in. They would have to be plugged in somewhere, and that would mean that some other cord would have to be unplugged. Getting everything back in place each time the forger finished a night's work would be dauntingly difficult.

Since it would surely be impossible for an artist to copy any large picture accurately from memory, perhaps photography came into the equation in some way. But even with the excellent color films that we have now, would a photograph furnish the forger with all he needed? Well, we were dealing with someone who was very clever. Either he could do it with a photograph, or I was missing something.

It was puzzling, and yet the substitution had been made. Therefore, it had been possible.

I tried to forget the whole thing—kept telling myself that I was under no obligation in this matter. But during the next few days the problem kept coming back to me. Sometimes I would wake up at night and find that the mystery was on my mind. Sometimes I felt a vague frustration, which I attributed to the fact that I saw no solution to the puzzle. At other times I would feel definitely distraught over the loss of a "million-dollar" painting.

A million dollars! What was it like to own something worth a million dollars? Just one object worth a million dollars! Of course we would never have sold the Louis-Philippe portrait. At least I don't think we would. Mrs. Chamberlain did not leave it to us to sell. She left it to us to keep and to show to the people of this area.

If we regained the picture, would it prove to be a useless gift? No, not if some Appalachian child saw it and ever after could say: "The King of France once came to our mountains. He didn't go to Kansas City or Chicago or L.A. or Seattle, or any of those places. He came right here to where we live." Isn't that worth something?

On the other hand, it was tempting to consider what the Historical Society could do with a million: build a museum; finance the restoration of a historic building?

I suppose that I could have gone on forever with thoughts of what might have been. But something happened that eventually shed light on everything.

The Murder of Randy Hartwell

HELEN DELAPORTE

Almost two weeks after we discovered that the portrait of
Louis-Philippe in our possession was a forgery, our small
city was shaken by a sensational occurrence. I saved the
clipping from the *Banner-Democrat*. Here it is:

BORDERVILLE MUSICIAN/ARTIST STABBED IN PALATIAL LIVING ROOM

The nude body of Randol Hartwell, stabbed
with an ornamental dagger, was found in his
palatial living room at 1225 Armadale Drive,
Borderville, Tenn., shortly after five o'clock yes-
terday afternoon by Charles Gunn of Gunn's
Flower Shop.

Gunn, a friend of the murdered man, had
dropped by to pick up bathing trunks he had left
behind after a pool party the evening before.
Finding Hartwell's car in the carport and the
kitchen door unlocked, his suspicions were
aroused when Hartwell did not respond to the
bell. Upon entering the house, Gunn found
Hartwell's totally nude body in a pool of blood

on the luxurious Oriental carpet of the dead man's elegantly appointed living room.

Emotionally distraught, Gunn told the *Banner-Democrat:* "There was blood everywhere. It was just terrible." City Detective Don Cochran declined to make any statement at this time, but it is rumored that police are seeking the identity of a mysterious overnight guest.

Well known to lovers of art and music in this area, Hartwell was often termed a Renaissance man, who had studied with the foremost piano virtuosi of Europe. He concertized widely in France and England before returning to his native Borderville to extend his artistic interests in other directions.

Randol Hartwell, "Randy" to his friends, was born Nov. 2, 1941, the son of the late Mr. and Mrs. G. W. Hartwell. He attended Cherry Street Elementary School and graduated from John Sevier High School in 1959. Before going to France for advanced study of the piano, Hartwell was the pupil of Arthur Paden of this city. He will be remembered locally for his countless musical soirees, attended by the cultural elite of this area.

Let the reader beware. Public statements about the dead, though generally correct as to fact, by omission often produce a cosmetic effect very similar to that the undertaker produces on the corpse itself.

Randol Hartwell was an old young man, self-conceived as a kind of universal genius. His pianistic technique was faulty and his repertoire modest. But what he played, he played with verve. If the listener did not insist on accuracy, the effect was impressive.

In addition to playing the piano, he pursued all the arts not only as collector but as practitioner. On one occasion when I was in his house, I was informed that most of the paintings on his walls were his own productions. I was also told that while in Europe he had continued his study of the dance, begun while a high school student, a fact backed by a framed photo of the adult Randy in leotard. But something about a tendon had made him give it up.

If one took Randy Hartwell at face value, he would seem to be a multitalented soul of impeccable artistic background. He was apparently affluent and came of a well-known Borderville family. No one would ever connect him with the disappearance of our portrait of Louis-Philippe.

And indeed I would never have thought of it myself. I knew the man only superficially. I did not find his personality attractive, and I am sure he saw little to regard in me. Randy's musical pretensions were exaggerated, but I felt that they were harmless.

Randy's position as a musician in our town was curious. It was clear to us that he placed himself on a professionally higher plane than the rest of us. He never participated in the affairs of the Borderville Music Club and rarely came to our recitals. If a concert artist came to town, he never attended unless the performer was acquainted, perhaps tenuously, with someone with whom Randy was also tenuously acquainted. Though he set himself up principally as a musician, he isolated himself in a kind of Olympian grandeur.

The pose he assumed was such that it would never have occurred to me to suspect him in connection with our stolen portrait. The connection, however, was made for me on the Sunday immediately following Randy's murder.

I had played a big postlude, stretching the capacity of Saint Luke's Hillgreen and Lane organ to the limit. I pressed the red button to turn the instrument off. Another service was over, and I was about to gather up my music and go down to the choir room, when I was aware of a small presence at my elbow: Frances Vogelsang.

It was déjà vu.

Those who have read *The Famous DAR Murder Mystery* may remember that this same little Frances Vogelsang came to me then in exactly the same way and gave me the information that explained why Luís García Valera happened to come to Borderville, and it was her information that led us at length to discover why he was murdered.

It is not surprising that someone would eventually give us the hint that would put us on the right track in the search for our painting. In a town the size of Borderville, *somebody* is bound to remember a scrap of information that will provide the key to any puzzle. And *somebody* is bound to put a fact and a suspicion together and hit the target dead center. But that Frances Vogelsang should be the woman who did it twice would be incredible to me if I did not know better.

Here is what happened:

I said, "Hello, Frances, how have you been?"

"I've been reading about *you.*"

"Oh, that was two weeks ago," I replied, almost ashamed of my notoriety.

"It was a good piece," she declared. "Is the Historical Society really going to give a reward to the one that has information that'll lead to you folks getting that picture back?"

"I guess that depends on the information," I said. With my music collected, I closed the organ and started to slide off the bench.

"And who do I give the information to? You?"

I stopped and gave Frances a surprised look.

"Well—yes."

With a very knowing expression in her eye, she said, "Randy Hartwell used to play at Mrs. Chamberlain's musical teas."

I was puzzled to see how this fact linked Randy with the theft.

Frances continued, "He was around that house quite a bit. He had his own key. I saw him use it."

Suddenly it hit me. That would have been long before he bought the Boesendorfer concert grand—Randy would have been willing enough to perform on Alberta Chamberlain's Steinway and be fawned over by elderly ladies at her "musical afternoons." Of course he would want to practice on that piano in the Chamberlains' aristocratic living room. And the sight of a young man letting himself into the Chamberlain house with his own key was precisely the kind of incident that would lodge in the mind of a woman like Frances Vogelsang.

Although her information contained no evidence whatever connecting Randy with the missing picture, I had a feeling—I really did—that Frances Vogelsang would eventually collect the $500 reward we were offering. And in fact she did.

George Hartwell and His Family

ROBERT KELSEY

Little pitchers have big ears. At least that was what they said about me when I was a little pitcher.

Mama was a widow and taught school to support me and my older brother, so we lived with my grandparents.

Grandma Walters was a real live wire. She knew everything about everybody all up and down the valley. And with my big ears I listened to everything she said. I guess that is where I got my interest in our own history right here in the Holston Valley. You see, there was nothing that ever happened here that didn't happen to somebody who was kin to somebody Grandma knew.

And then, of course, when I went to work at the post office, I got to know lots of folks. You might say I am a specialist in the folks that live around here.

That is why Mrs. Delaporte wants me to write what I know about Randy Hartwell and his family.

I asked her, "Do I have to tell *all*? There won't be any space for the other folks to write in this book if I do."

She didn't think she wanted that much. Just enough for a background—enough to explain Randy.

But none of us could ever explain Randy.

He was what I call heat lightning. That's something to

watch on a summer evening when you don't have anything better to do. It's something to look at, but it never amounts to much.

Seeing that I live just two blocks from Randy's place, I have amused myself for years just observing his doings. But I'm no closer to explaining Randy Hartwell than I was when I commenced. How in the world could Randy Hartwell come from such a plain, everyday family as the Hartwells? But Mrs. Delaporte wants me to explain him, and I'll sure as hell try.

As far back as anyone remembers, the Kelseys and the Hartwells lived near each other on the Virginia side of the border down near Brown Spring.

It's a wonder none of the Kelseys ever married any of the Hartwells. In all the years the two families lived out there, you would expect at least one marriage between them. But it never happened. Now, there was nothing wrong with the Hartwells. I don't mean to say there was. They were good folks. But they were Christians—that's Disciples of Christ—and we were Methodists.

Hartwells were all hardworking and thrifty. But George Hartwell's father, Adam Hartwell, had just too many children. And as they came along and grew up, he didn't have the money to help each one in the way he might have liked.

The girls, of course, got married, and that took care of them. And the boys turned out well, too. But George had something in him that made him different from the rest. He was a go-getter who wouldn't wait for anybody.

This was all before my time, but I remember Grandma talking about how she knew George when he walked the country roads barefoot to save his shoes.

George started out with a pack on his back selling baking powder, vanilla extract, and Wine of Carduai. That last item was for what we used to call "women's complaint." If a shot of bourbon was what a churchgoing lady really needed, Wine of Carduai was a mighty good substitute.

Roads in the country were not good back then, and in a wet spell country women couldn't get to the store. Most of the things we ate were grown on the place, but a woman needed baking powder and vanilla extract, and it was bad when those things ran low—and the Wine of Carduai was such a blessing that the womenfolk just couldn't do without it.

What I'm building up to is that George was able to buy a spring wagon pretty soon. He painted his name on the side of that wagon and added buckets and tubs, mops, brooms, flatirons, and a few other things to his line. Mr. Hartwell gave George a spavined old horse, and George and his horse and all his wares went up and down the ways and the byways all over our part of the valley.

He was very accommodating: if a lady wanted a certain item that George did not carry, she just had to mention it, and George would bring it to her the next time he passed her house.

For a bachelor, he was doing very well—specially a bachelor no older than twenty-one or twenty-two. But one of the Hunsucker girls took his eye. He wanted to marry her, and her daddy wasn't pleased to think of a son-in-law who peddled his wares from a wagon—even one with the owner's name painted on the side.

But George could always read the cards right, and he decided to make himself into a real merchant. He rented a small store here in Borderville at the other end of town from the railroad station and added kitchen ranges, cooking paraphernalia, kitchen cabinets, chairs and tables, and washing machines, which were beginning to be popular with town ladies.

All the women who used to buy his Wine of Carduai remembered him and visited his shop whenever they were in town.

George was polite, ready to serve, and willing to take the least possible profit. Finally he felt that he was really in business and making good. He was ready to show old man Hunsucker the sign over his shop that said GEORGE W. HARTWELL. EVERYTHING FOR THE KITCHEN. Hunsucker gave in, and George married Rachel. Their first boy came along the next year.

Meanwhile George had found that living married in town was a good deal more expensive than he could have imagined.

About that time the store next to his went out of business. George got a loan from the bank, rented the vacant shop, opened a large arch between it and his original place, and put in a line of household furniture of all sorts.

It was cheap stuff. It was the cheapest furniture to be had for forty or fifty miles on either side of the border. Grandma had a sofa bed that came from George Hartwell's store. It was the ugliest old thing and almighty uncomfortable, but it was what she could afford. Seeing that there were lots of folks like Grandma, George was soon doing all right.

And it was a good thing, because by that time he had four boys. From the oldest to the least they were Myron, Hunsucker (called Hunny), Woodrow, and Jim. I imagine they were just as hard on shoes and other clothes as most boys are, and that was all the more reason for George to go right ahead with his business.

He rented a larger store up toward the station and got a better line of merchandise. He was a deacon in Central Christian Church and a charter member of the Kiwanis Club.

They always say you can take a boy out of the country but you can't take the country out of the boy. Whoever thought that up must have known George Hartwell.

Of course the Brown-Spring connection didn't hurt George at all, but he knew there was something he didn't have and never would have. And the Lord knows Rachel didn't have it, either. She was just a plain, honest woman, but she would never have any idea about furniture aside from sitting on it, lying down on it, or eating off of it.

George decided his store needed more class.

Of course it did.

So he hired himself an interior decorator. She was Nettie Marie Threadgil from Roanoke. I don't know just how she learned to be a decorator, but she had ideas about things.

That was in the twenties, when business was looking up everywhere. After one or two ladies had got Miss Threadgil to do their living rooms over, here came all the rest. Hiring Nettie Marie turned out to be one of the best moves George Hartwell ever made.

The Hartwell boys were all in their teens and early twenties by the time Rachel, their mother, turned poorly. I don't know what she died of, but she had it for a good while. I remember the women would lower their voices when they talked about it. So it must have been cancer in some part of the body that people didn't mention in those days. She died sometime during the Depression.

Like anyone in those days, George saw his business go down quite a bit, but he came out of it better than most. He must have had something salted away, and with deflation, that carried him through. So there he was, a widower and not strapped for money.

Of course with the Depression, folks thought they could get along without interior or any other kind of decorating. But Nettie Marie worked in sales there in the store, and the ladies thought that if Nettie Marie waited on them, they were getting the benefit of "interior decorating" without paying for it. Then one day George and Nettie Marie surprised everybody by getting married.

Right after the wedding, people began to see a change in George. In those days a man who owned a store would naturally wear a white shirt and a suit. But Nettie Marie saw to it that he wore a tie that went with the suit and socks that matched his shoes. I imagine she began buying his clothes for him right away. At any rate, everything he wore was a good fit and pressed just right. You wouldn't think that he had grown up on the farm, he looked so fine.

When it comes to the boys, I don't know what they thought about their new stepmother. I do know that they got out of the house mighty quick. But only one of them married. That was Myron. He married Margie Dunlap, and they had one daughter, Jessie Anne, that married Chris Shankley. Myron is dead, and so are Jessie Anne and Chris. But Jessie left a little boy for her mother, Margie, to bring up. There will be more about him later.

To get back to Nettie Marie and George, there was quite some difference in age between them. But along about 1942 Nettie Marie presented George with another son—Randol, the one everyone called Randy—the one that was murdered last year.

I remember how surprised I was when I got home from the war to find that old George Hartwell had a baby boy at his house, because the boys by the first marriage were all older than I was, and here George had a kid young enough to have been mine.

As you see, the ages in that family were all mixed up. George was about sixty-five, Nettie Marie might have been forty, the boys of the first marriage would have been something between twenty-eight to thirty-eight, and then there was Randy, who was about two.

Now, I have heard it said that George was a downright fool about the baby—Randy, our Randol Hartwell that this book is about. When Randy was around ten years old, I thought George was in his dotage. Of course he wasn't more than five years older than I am now. However that may be, it was natural that he would die long before Nettie Marie. She was bound to live a good bit longer than he would, and of course there was Randy to be reared and educated.

All the same, it was a shock to the older boys when their pappy died and left everything to Nettie Marie and nothing to them. They did their best to break the will, but none of them was as mad about it as Myron's wife, Margie. If there was ever any chance of reconciling the two families, she saw to it that it never took place.

Now that's the family history of the Hartwells. As I have said, the four sons by the first marriage are dead; so is Nettie Marie. That means that the only members of the clan that were living when our story began were Randy, Margie, and her grandson, James Budworth Shankley, who, because he runs his two given names together when he says them, was called at first "Spudworth," and then simply "Spud."

I am going to leave it here and let Mrs. Bushrow try to explain about Nettie Marie and how she raised Randy.

Nettie Marie and Her Boy Randy

HARRIET GARDNER BUSHROW

Helen Delaporte has asked me to write up what I know about Nettie Marie Hartwell and that precious Randy of hers.

Well, yes indeed! I knew Nettie Marie—knew her better than I wanted to know her. Nettie Marie got mad over something at the Christian church and decided to join the Presbyterians. You may have noticed that when anybody pulls out of one church and goes off to another, she sometimes throws herself into everything at the new church just to show the other people how much they lost when she left. But the steam runs out after a while. And that's all right. It's hard enough to get anybody to do church work anyhow. I won't make a very close inspection as to motives.

Of course, ten years later Nettie Marie got mad at us and joined the Lutherans. But I can tell you something about her while she was with us.

That poor girl didn't really know who she was, if you understand what I mean. Now, take me. From the time that I knew anything, I knew I was a Gardner and that my mother was a Hadley. That meant, of course, that I had certain privileges, but it also meant that there were obligations. If I didn't like the last half of that proposition, I certainly made the most of the other. And I am still here at ninety.

But Nettie Marie didn't have any of that. She had a certain amount of money—from her husband, you see—and she saw that as privilege, but she didn't know anything about the obligation that went along with it.

Nettie Marie came here from Roanoke. I don't know how many people from Roanoke I have asked, and not one of them knew anything about her.

Now that's a pity, and I shouldn't hold a thing like that against her. I know plenty of people from very modest families that never let it make a bit of difference to them in any way. And they are just as fine as anybody else.

With Nettie Marie, I am afraid, it was altogether different. Somehow she always had to prove herself. I'm pretty sure that's why she went into interior decorating, because people who hire a decorator have to be admitting that the decorator has better taste; and Nettie Marie could tell them just what to do.

Of course, interior decorating has come a long way from what Nettie Marie used to do. Nowadays, decorators bring a lot more to the business—courses in design schools—so many things they have to know, so many books on the subject, and so on. So it's very different today.

Now being a Gardner and a Hadley, I inherited a good deal of my furniture, which wasn't considered stylish back in the twenties. But mine were family things, and I wasn't about to clear out the house and buy new stuff. So I didn't know much about Nettie Marie until she decided to be a Presbyterian. Of course I knew she didn't have just my taste, and that was about it.

After Lamar and I came back to Borderville in the fifties, I helped out in the Sunday School. I had a class of girls in the Intermediate Department. You know how it used to be. We had all the children in the department come together for "opening exercises," sing little songs, celebrate birthdays, take up the collection, and so on. Then we took the children to separate classes—boys in one class and girls in another for each grade in school. Back in those days the children preferred it that way.

I'm glad I had a class of girls. That meant I didn't have to deal with Randy Hartwell every week. But in the department I had plenty of opportunity to watch that boy and to observe his mother, too.

The reason Randy turned out to be the way he was was nothing more nor less than Nettie Marie. That boy never heard his mother say a word that didn't indicate that he was absolutely perfect—except for his health. She was forever worrying about it, though I never saw anything wrong with him in that line.

She started Randy studying the piano with Mr. Paden when the boy was only six years old. By the time he was in the Intermediate Department, she was constantly pushing to have him play his new piece during the opening exercises. She said the experience was so necessary because he was going to be a concert artist. Then the next minute she would tell us how he said he just wanted to share his talent with others.

When it came time for a Christmas or an Easter pageant, we teachers were worried to death with telephone calls about how we could best avail ourselves of Master Randy's talents. Then, when we gave the child the best part, she would have a costume made for him that laid the rest of the costumes in the shade, and the other children would just look shabby alongside Randy.

There were recitations he had to give, and I can't begin to tell all the ways that boy had to show off. Some of the girls thought he was cute, but the boys couldn't stand him.

Now, about Randy's health: Nettie Marie just made a career of it! If the weather was cold, she wrapped the boy in sweaters and coats and mufflers. If it rained, Randy showed up with umbrella, rain hat, raincoat, and overshoes. I could never get Lamar, Jr., to wear a hat, let alone galoshes, or to carry an umbrella.

And then there were the vitamins. If Randy got a runny nose, she told us all about the treatment. Of course she was the main financial support of the pediatrician. I feel sure that he saw what was going on. So he advised exercise, thinking that would be baseball or something on that order. But Nettie Marie was afraid Randy would hurt his hands somehow, and just think what that would do to his career as a concert pianist! But exercise he must have.

That's how he got into the ballet lessons.

I guess maybe it was good exercise. I'll say this, though: the child would have been better off wading in the creek, climbing trees, falling out at least once and breaking an arm. A few fights with boys his own age would have helped him—mostly, I guess, because that could only happen when he was out of Nettie Marie's sight.

Of course we had to hear all about the ballet. Nettie Marie got into a regular dither; she didn't know whether Randy should be the world's greatest piano player or the greatest dancer.

There was something else that came into focus about that time and would show up again and again: Randy was forever giving presents. Of course, that isn't quite the way it was. Randy didn't give the presents. His mother gave them—paying a kind of insurance, don't you see, because it would be mighty hard to say no next time if you still had your purse with the pretty little handkerchief that you received the last time you let Randy have the biggest part in the performance.

I don't know whether the woman coached him or

whether Randy had a natural way with him, but he could make a little speech when he presented his gift that would lead you to think he was Sir Walter Raleigh spreading out his coat over a mud puddle so you could walk on it.

There is no question that the boy was his mother's true son, and they certainly agreed on one thing: that Master Randol Hartwell was an absolute genius and the bright star of the universe. No doubt every child has a natural tendency to see himself in that light, but Nettie Marie groomed Randy and pushed him and cultivated that ambitious stripe in his character like an expert growing rare orchids or something similar. She said she was going to make a Renaissance man of him. Said it to everybody. And that's how he got the reputation.

Well, Helen wanted me to explain how Randy got to be the way he was. Perhaps you have some idea about that now.

My Student Who Would Not Count

ARTHUR PADEN

I have a vivid memory of the first time I ever saw Randy
Hartwell. In fact, I have a vivid memory of almost everything that ever involved Randy, his mother, and me.

Randy was six years old when Mrs. Hartwell came to me
for advice. She had on a gray wool suit with a pink blouse.
Her rouge and nail polish exactly matched the blouse. She
also wore a gray fox fur.

The boy was in a blue suit, and there was a neatly folded
little handkerchief showing its points out of the breast
pocket of the jacket.

During my time as a piano teacher, I have dealt with hundreds of mothers and their budding Rubinsteins. They
come to my studio, usually in street clothes, though now I
am not at all surprised to see a mother in a warm-up suit.
Randy Hartwell's mother, however, was paying a state visit.
For that matter, she never paid any other kind.

To a mother who wants to know when her child should
begin piano lessons, most teachers will say: "After he has
learned to read." But of course there was Mozart.

I look at the hand; then, if it is developed enough for the
child to play with comfort the intervals he will find in the

first-year book, and if the child expresses a desire to learn, I take him at that point.

If I gave marks for appearance and deportment, Randy Hartwell would certainly be the best student I ever had. He always came to his lesson on time in what appeared to be his best clothes. His hair was always neatly combed and looked fresh from the barber. He seemed to listen politely to what I told him. But I could not get him to count.

He developed a nice touch and had a flair for dynamics. He always expressed maximum enthusiasm for whatever piece I assigned him. He learned his pieces—even got 98 percent of the notes right and had all the confidence in the world. But I simply could not get him to count.

Mrs. Hartwell's sense of rhythm seemed also to have been somewhat deficient. At least once a month she would tell me what pleasure it was to hear Randol practice.

It nearly drove me mad. Many times I thought I would tell the woman to discontinue the lessons. But she had put me under obligation. She brought me a plaster bust of Beethoven, which I was pleased enough to get. She brought me a pair of brass candlesticks and said they would be ideal on my mantelpiece. Whenever I presented my students in recital, she brought punch and cookies. At the last lesson before Christmas, Randy always came into the studio with a tin of fruitcake and a flask of Chianti.

I received smoked turkeys, Virginia hams, even a dressing gown. I can't name it all. After three or four years of that kind of thing, it is impossible to tell a mother: "Madam, your son has a certain talent—not at all unusual—and could become a tolerable performer. But since he refuses to follow instructions, regretfully I cannot teach him any longer."

From time to time I would steel myself to make just that declaration. But then there would be a recital, and Randy would exceed his own ability. The lapses of rhythm in his performance remained. And yet there was an element of élan far beyond anything to be expected at his age. His audiences always applauded him extravagantly.

A thing like that is very hard on the teacher. It undercuts him. After the poor man has said a hundred times, "If you don't count, you'll never be able to play," the kid gets up in front of twenty-five grownups, makes every mistake you've been warning him against for two months but does it with the assurance of a Paderewski—and what happens? Applause. No other kid's applause comes anywhere near it.

But then there is the annual competition. Randy would play in such a competition and the judge's comment would come back: "Ragged rhythm!"

Now he'll quit, I thought.

To my surprise, Randy took the criticism calmly. The bland expression on his self-confident little face did not change at all. He paid no more attention to the judges than he did to me. He was the most exasperating kid I ever saw. I dreaded his lessons as much as he seemed to enjoy them.

Eventually and inevitably, Randy was in high school. He *did* have talent—enough talent for what? Concert work? I was convinced not. Accompaniment? Not likely. The star does not accompany anybody. Teaching? God forbid.

But now that he was in his teens, we had to look ahead. I had very serious talks with Randy. As always, he listened with that serene facial expression that never betrayed his thoughts.

Mrs. Hartwell was as confident of Randy's bright future as ever. But she was just as confident of Randy's "other talents." "That boy writes such sensitive poems," she would confide. Apparently she expected poetry to fill the idle hours between concert engagements. She also mentioned

Randy's ballet lessons and became very excited when Randy had a part in the annual presentation of *The Nutcracker.* I suggested that Randy's true metier might well lie in the dance. But Mrs. Hartwell remained faithful to her first determination: Randy had been dedicated to the piano, and piano it must be.

At last Randy arrived at his final year in high school. I was determined to try once more to have a serious talk with him.

"Do you expect to continue with the piano after you graduate?" I asked.

"Oh yes." He said it as though he had never entertained any other notion.

"Well, you know you can't continue to study with me," I said.

Randy looked away. I feel sure he had entertained visions of advanced study in which I would play no part. But he probably had not realized how soon that would be.

"What are you going to do?" I pressed.

No answer.

"Have you chosen a college?"

There was a shake of the head.

"Will you continue with the piano in college?"

"Oh yes."

For the first time I felt that I was getting through to Randy.

"You know you are not really prepared for advanced study."

This was a shock to Randy. The criticisms of the judges in all those competitions had had no effect. The adulation he received from his mother simply washed them out.

I felt almost guilty. It was late for me to be saying these things. I should have said them long before. But had I not shouted, "Count! Count! Count!"

"We will enter you in the spring competition," I told him. "It draws entrants from as far away as Bluefield and Galax. If you do well, you can perhaps major in piano to some purpose. Otherwise I would suggest that you get a degree in business administration or something else in which you can expect to do well."

I was presenting Randy with a view of reality that had never occurred to him.

"You really want to go on with piano?" I asked.

"Oh yes."

"You want to major in music?"

"Yes."

"If you will do exactly what I say—practice very hard and count *while you are practicing*—give up ballet and whatever else takes up your time and concentrate on your piano," I promised, "there is some possibility that you might become a professional musician."

Randy vowed that he would tell his mother all that I had said and comply to the letter with all my instructions.

There was a marked improvement in the lessons. And when Randy did not appear that Christmas in *The Nutcracker*, I had glimmers of hope. I actually did.

But eight months is an eternity for an adolescent. And the distractions of the senior year in a modern high school are a major impediment to any serious effort. I grant that Randy tried—tried as hard as I could have expected of any teenager.

I was pleased with his progress. There was no miracle, but there was conspicuous improvement. When the judges returned their criticism to us, it was good. Good enough, in fact, that Nettie Marie Hartwell could elevate it in her own mind to something extraordinary. Her darling's superiority had been vindicated and I was the best of all teachers. Of course, I could not very well contradict her.

I learned through my wife that Mrs. H. was telling her acquaintances that she was now thinking of European study for her young genius.

Such a project was preposterous on any count. The day when European study was obligatory for American artists ended some decades ago. We now have excellent music schools and excellent departments of music in our colleges and universities, where there is instruction equivalent to anything offered elsewhere in the world. The notion that Randy was ready to study at an advanced level was laughable, but the idea that he would have to cross the Atlantic to find instruction commensurate with his talent was more than laughable: it was outrageous. His mother, however, was obsessive. The reality of the case meant nothing to her.

Thank heaven, I was prepared for what she would say when she came to me.

She brought Randy with her, and they had a package wrapped in white tissue paper and tied with narrow, dark blue ribbon. The woman, after a fashion, had some sense of style.

When I got the paper off the thing, it was an eight-by-ten-inch portrait of Randy in a silver frame. Across the lower right-hand corner was written: "To Arthur Paden, with appreciation for his encouragement and sensitive instruction."

I was speechless—not through any sudden recognition of unexpected gratitude but out of the very enormity of the thing. The silver frame, the inscription: they were calculated to put me under obligation. I was confounded. That woman had the upper hand.

"We have decided," she said, as though she had consulted Randy in the matter—and I suppose she actually thought she had—"we have decided that Randy should go straight on to Europe for further study."

It was like a speech from a novel or a play. If it had not been so grotesque, it would have been funny. All I could think of to say was: "Yes?"

"I hope you don't think we undervalue your teaching," she continued, "but as you have said to Randol several times this past year, he has reached that stage in his playing where he must go on to some other teacher."

This was apparently the version she had heard from Randy.

"I think it best," I said meekly.

"That is why we are here. We need your advice—about the maestro."

The maestro! Where did the woman get such ideas?

"Where should Randy study?" she pursued. "In France? He speaks French, you know—took it all four years in high school."

I suppose John Sevier High has as good a French department as may be expected, but I doubt that Randy's fluency equaled his mother's confidence therein.

So France it was to be!

"If you would give us the names of two or three maestros," she said, "so that we can choose, you know—we would appreciate it so much."

I was floored. I said I would make inquiries and let her know something in a week or two.

Fortunately—or unfortunately, as the case may be—my wife has a cousin who is a technician with UIA in Paris. I wrote to Glenn asking for the names of several piano teachers in Paris or its environs. I explained that the student who would be coming was of dubious promise, all things considered, and that I would not inflict Randy on anyone of reputation.

I don't know how Glenn got the list of names that he sent me. He is a "technician," a word I have always associated with efficiency. Nevertheless, I was somewhat surprised to receive a prompt answer to my query. Glenn had provided three names, each with an address; after one of the names he had noted: "This one comes nearest to speaking English." I turned the list over to Mrs. Hartwell and washed my hands of the matter.

It was the teacher whose English was least bad who won the prize. M. Josef Armand sent abundant information—information about tuition, practice pianos, living accommodations, the works—in words that needed interpretation but not translation. Randy's trunk and supplies such as record player, library of LPs, and other paraphernalia necessary to the life of a young aesthete were sent over well in advance. In September, when contemporaries were going off to their colleges, Randy himself "embarked" at Three City Airport for the culture and excitement of the "City of Light."

He flew home for a week at Christmas. When he called on me, he told me that M. Armand had praised his preparation and pronounced me a superior instructor, which story, if it was true, should have roused my suspicion immediately. I, however, felt sure the message was a lie from beginning to end, concocted by Randy to prove that my estimate of him had been wrong.

It was apparent that foreign study had benefitted Randy in at least one way. It had freed him from the cloying adoration of his mother. That his ego continued to be fed by the flattery of M. Armand seemed likely, however. Otherwise, I do not think he would have returned to that "maestro."

For three years Randy paid only infrequent and brief visits to Borderville. Sometimes he saw me; sometimes he did not. His mother, on the other hand, called me every time she received a letter from Paris. I heard all the details.

Randy played at recitals, which in his mother's retelling became engagements and concerts. The woman was utterly insane on the subject of her boy.

Finally Randy returned, more or less to maintain a base in Borderville.

He played on various occasions in Borderville. I received no special invitation, though I attended once or twice. He played exactly as he had done before he went to Europe. He did not ask for my criticism of those few performances that I heard.

Whatever else Randy may have learned in Paris, he learned how to put on a very good imitation of a bon vivant. He spent lots of money. We were a little surprised that he had the wherewithal to support his adopted lifestyle. Nevertheless, what he was doing seemed to serve his purpose. As opposed to a drudge of a musician, I fear the world prefers and admires the bon vivant.

Well! Poor Randy has been murdered. I woke in the night about a week ago asking myself to what extent I was responsible for what happened in his life. The boy had been in my hands for—good heavens!—twelve years, committed to me for a certain kind of discipline. And I had not given it to him. If I had only convinced him of the validity of that maxim so often repeated to me by my grandmother, "There is no excellence without great labor," would his life have been better? Would he have escaped murder—naked, they say, with an ornamental dagger in his back? I feel a strong sense of regret.

But I yelled at him often enough. I yelled, "Count!"

Michael Ferrin's Letter

HELEN DELAPORTE

No, I don't know everyone in the world, although some people swear that I do. But, as one of my friends says, there are only two hundred people in the world.

That is not true, of course, but I operate on the basis that the two hundred people I know in turn know two hundred people—and so, as the circle widens, somewhere among those acquaintances and their acquaintances there is bound to be someone out there to whom I can apply politely and explain my need, who can then put me in touch with just about anybody.

The loss of a million-dollar portrait belonging to a Society for which I have some responsibility seems to me a circumstance dire enough to justify activating the whole fuse box controlling my acquaintances, charging all lines wherever they may connect, and thus putting the two-hundred-people-in-the-world theory to the test. I determined to do just that.

The reader no doubt remembers that little Mrs. Vogelsang gave me the hint at church only a few days after the Hartwell murder that Randol Hartwell had had access to Mrs. Chamberlain's house some years ago; and from that fact both Mrs. Vogelsang and I immediately jumped to the conclusion that Randy Hartwell, if not the sole perpetrator, was very much involved in the theft of our painting.

If the reader will be patient, he/she will shortly understand that our assumption was perfectly natural, given the character attributed to Randy by quite a number of Bordervillians; and, further, he/she will shortly learn how we gained proof that we were right.

But in the meantime the orderly presentation of our story requires a somewhat chronological examination of the character, experience, and proclivities of Mr. Randol Hartwell.

And that is where my two hundred friends and *their* two hundred friends enter the story.

I am an organist with an M.A. degree in music from the Eastman School of Music. I am not a famous artist, but I know an awful lot of professional musicians—shared student days or studied under them at Eastman or met them at regional or national American Guild of Organists / AGO meetings. And while the Southern mountains are mere Dogpatch in the eyes of the rest of the nation, let me tell you that we have three excellent pipe organs in Borderville—instruments on which the finest organists in the world could play without apology. And first-rate organists do in fact come to us with recitals. When they do, I entertain them at my house or I am a dinner guest when they are entertained at some other place. As a result of all this, I think that I probably know people who would know or could find out about any other musician in the world.

The friend to whom I resorted for information this time was Mike Ferrin. Mike is on the music faculty at Saint Dunstan's in Nova Scotia. Some twenty years ago—no, it would be thirty years ago—he studied with Langlais in Paris. That would be about the same time that Randy Hartwell was there.

I felt certain that Americans in Paris—musical Americans, that is—in the same period of two or three years would run into each other over and over. They would, if nothing else, occupy the cheapest seats at the most desirable musical events because attending such events is one of the reasons they are in Paris.

I wrote to Mike, explaining my interest in Randy Hartwell and asking Mike what he might know. I didn't hear for three weeks. But then I received an envelope containing a covering letter from Mike explaining that he had forwarded my query to a friend—a music student who had married a Frenchman and remained in Paris—who he thought might know about Randy. With it he enclosed the reply that the friend had sent to Mike. That letter follows:

Dear Mike,

Great to hear from you. We should really keep up with each other, but somehow it just doesn't happen.

Matter of fact—your friend's request is very interesting. Yes, I knew Randy Hartwell. Wouldn't want to call him a friend, but knew a good bit about him. He got to be a kind of joke with some of my crowd. He ran around pretending to be a serious student. "Studied"—note the quotation marks—with Armand; and that's what makes Randy Hartwell interesting.

You say he has been murdered! That is sad, but I can't resist the temptation to observe that he would probably have preferred that to some private, ordinary death.

All right—here's the dope. Josef Armand, the teacher about whom your friend wishes to know, was a motheaten, rotund number with a fiercely black mustache and a wisp or two of dyed hair across his bald pate. I saw him only once or twice—at musical events, you understand. But on those occasions there was a very strong aroma of alcohol about him, which is probably the reason he was reduced to accepting into his class anyone who came to him. If the thing had been otherwise, Randy would never have had a chance.

All the same, I got the idea that old Armand had been a person of some promise at one time. The musical establishment seemed to know him and treated him with a kind of charitable condescension. You know the stuff—"Poor old Josef, too bad about him!"

Nevertheless, his past connections made it possible for him to go—with his students—where there would be a few musicians of the first quality, the old fraternity sort of thing. And a performer of moderately high standing would see him and say, "Josef! So good to see you! When are you going to play for us again?" and then turn away before "Josef" could reply.

I think you get the idea. Randy Hartwell's musical studies were a joke.

And we would have dismissed Randy along with his teacher except that Randy was so absolutely fascinating to watch.

He seemed to have some notion of Paris as it was in the twenties and was determined to follow the pattern. He scattered money around, and we thought he must be rich, but nobody really knew.

He had an attic apartment—on the Left Bank, naturally. I was there just one time. The stairs to the place were filthy. But once across the threshold, the contrast was a shock: Everything in perfect order—*objets de vertu*—from the flea market, no doubt, but certainly better stuff than you would expect.

No—I won't say that. In a way it was what I should have expected. Although Randy was doing his best to be Bohemian, he just never looked the part. His gray trousers and blue blazer, his highly shined brown shoes, his white shirts with the silk rep ties—he was very careful about his looks. And his hair—light blond, very neat, straight—freshly trimmed. He was a good-looking kid. In fact, too good-looking.

Unmarried male musicians, as I am sure you know, run the strong risk of being thought gay. The example of Liszt or Chopin, and a good many others, ought to throw the suspicion the other way, but it doesn't. Well, what about Randy?

He was young, slender, had that smooth complexion and those blue eyes. I am not sure what attracts the homosexual, but apparently Randy had it, because we began to see him at the opera, etc., with a group that gave every indication of the gay lifestyle.

But imagine my surprise one evening at a performance of *Turandot* when I saw Randy in tails, sitting in a loge with a middle-aged man of apparent savoir faire. With my rented glasses I could look down into the loge. The gentleman's plump hand was resting on Randy's thigh.

After that, Randy was seen with other men of a certain age—all of them affluent.

I don't know how long Randy remained in Paris—I would guess no longer than three years. I did not know when he left, but it was before the scandal broke.

I wish I had saved the clipping. The story was sensational enough, however, that I remember it clearly.

Armand had been the kingpin in a ring of art thieves. He specialized in taking modern masters from the apartments of rich homosexuals. Armand's protégés, after becoming intimate with the middle-aged gentlemen, familiarized themselves with their possessions, learned the secrets of their security systems, if any, and obtained copies of the necessary keys. Then, while one of the gentlemen and his young lover were in Nice or Geneva, the old man's choice possessions would be quietly removed from his apartment.

There was no evidence that Randy was involved, but the news from your friend in Tennessee makes me think he surely must have been.

Anyhow, that's all I know about Randy Hartwell. From what you tell me about your friend's interest in Randy's activities, I would say that everything fits.

You didn't tell me anything about yourself. Are you concertizing?

One of Jean's compositions is to be recorded by the Suisse Romande. The children are doing well. Cecile is being married in September—a young violinist. René is organist at Saint-Antoine but is looking for a better place. I am quite the *maman*. I hardly ever play anymore. Jean is working on a new symphony. When it is completed,

we hope to make a quick trip to the States. Perhaps somehow we will be able to see you. That
would be so nice.

As ever,
Geraldine Drouet

Now I'll report what happened when Randy came back
from France.

His mother, of course, was atwitter. She gave him a wel-
come-home party in her house—the old G. W. Hartwell
home place on Bedford Street.

It was decorated in a pronounced personal taste. The
drapes were brown velvet with gold fringe. The rug was
Oriental. There was a camelback sofa and wing chairs rem-
iniscent of Chippendale, upholstered in a floral pattern.
The pictures were impressionist—several still lifes, as I remember. I took them to be expensive reproductions.

There was a very nice eight-foot Baldwin grand. From
the condition of the finish, I would say that the Hartwells
had bought it at the time Randy began his piano lessons.

I remember an absolutely huge bowl of mums and glad-
ioli on the coffee table. Elsewhere in the room there were
photographs of Randy at various stages of growth—all in
silver frames.

I made mildly complimentary comments on the appearance of the house.

"Oh, do you like it?" Mrs. Hartwell said, not as a question but as an acknowledgment of her professional skill. "I
imagine we will do it over rather soon," she proceeded.
"You know, Randy and I are opening my shop again when
the stock arrives. He selected it in France, and I can hardly
wait to see it."

That was the first but not the last time I heard about the
new Hartwell Interiors. It was surprising how often I met

Randy or Mrs. Hartwell in the next month—in town or at a program—and there was always much said about the shop.

"You must come as soon as we open," Nettie Marie would say. "I know you'll want to see the beautiful things Randy has selected."

I don't deny that there was a strong current of curiosity stirring among a certain set of Borderville women. Bear in mind that Randy was very good-looking and there was something in him that appealed to the maternal instinct of quite a number of our ladies.

At length a quarter-page ad in the *Banner-Democrat* announced the opening of Hartwell Interiors.

They rented a house—an older place spruced up to their specification. It was given new paint, the sagging porch was removed, and carriage lamps were added to the entrance, which was now protected by a stylish awning boldly striped in black and gold. It looked very smart with the new walk of old brick that led from the street and the topiary box-woods in the great terra-cotta urns at either side of the steps.

Of course I went to see it. And I must admit that Randy had picked up a lot of knowledge about taste and style—perhaps from the robbery victims of M. Armand, with whom Randy may or may not have had liaisons. But of course we had no notion of that sort of thing then.

I don't remember all the wares displayed at Hartwell Interiors, but I know there were porcelains, a Louis XIV globe, and many old books in morocco bindings. It seemed to me there was a sofa and two chairs of the Louis XV period. There were paintings, too—eighteenth century, not by artists whose names are likely to be known. But they looked like the paintings of other artists whose names *are* likely to be known.

All Borderville saw these treasures. There was much talk and some buying, but the demand for such wares in our particular corner of the world at that time was soon satisfied. It was not long until we were told by Nettie Marie that Randy was looking about with the idea of taking his collection to a larger place.

"He needs the city," she informed us, "so that he can have more scope."

Randy's choice settled upon Baltimore, where his European artifacts, no doubt, were more at home.

I don't remember how long he was in Maryland. After all, I never really knew Randy well, as I have admitted. I should think it was not more than a year or a year and a half. Nor did I know whether the shop succeeded or failed. Randy was still in his early twenties, you see; and it takes a great deal of experience, talent, and hard work to establish any business—not to mention the kind of competition to be expected in a place like Baltimore. Successful or not, Randy returned to Borderville when his mother was diagnosed with a serious cancer problem.

Randy was an exemplary son during the year or so that it took Nettie Marie to decline and die. He gave her every attention and truly earned the accolades of all his mother's circle.

There is no sadder time than the months one spends watching a parent sink slowly into death. I am sure it was melancholy for Randy. Consequently, it was a kindness of Alberta Chamberlain during Randy's vigil to ask him to perform at her charity teas. People observed that it was good for him—got him out of the house, gave him a chance to release his emotions in music, and so on.

When Nettie Marie died, Randy was not yet twenty-five years old. As her heir, he received what was left of the Hartwell fortune and Nettie Marie's insurance benefits as well. The older ladies of Borderville, with whom Randy had become quite a darling, wondered, "What next?"

What next, indeed! It wasn't what they expected. Randy went Bohemian—or as close to it as possible in a place like Borderville.

He never affected the look of the Left Bank, but he drew together all the arty types in the area and, I suppose, presided. Since the organist at an Episcopal church does not qualify for inclusion in such a group as Randy's, and since I am some fifteen years older than he, I am no expert as to his friends of that period.

There was one development, however, of which we were all aware: Pierre!

Pierre was French, and Randy's age. He painted, and perhaps because of Pierre, Randy took up painting also. He converted three of the rooms in his house to an art studio and gave showings, which I did not attend but about which I did hear.

At first it was thought that Pierre was Randy's gay lover. Pierre was in fact anything but gay. Exotic and good-looking, he was besieged by a number of impressionable girls; and Pierre responded—or perhaps I should use the more accurate word "pursued." And chiefly he pursued Gloria Gatewood, whose father was an official of Amalgamated Coal. Pierre and Gloria raced around town in her bright red convertible. It was generally expected that Pierre was going to marry a small fortune, when Gloria rammed the convertible into an abutment on the Virginia side of town. Both Pierre and Gloria were killed instantly.

There was much show of sympathy all round—to the Gatewoods, who had lost a daughter (although they had escaped a son-in-law), and to Randy, who had lost a friend.

Then it was discovered that Randy had insured his friend's life—some said for a hundred thousand dollars.

Not very frequently, but upon occasion, the two halves of our city agree on a project to improve the lives of all of us. Such a project was a "freeway" making it possible to travel from the southern boundary of Borderville, Tennessee, to the northern limit of Borderville, Virginia, almost in a straight line. This was a novelty, because our hilly terrain mostly determines where we are going to live and how we are going to arrange our streets.

I won't go into the details of engineering and financing, but it took years to make the plans. After various routes had been projected, publicized, criticized, and modified, at last a victorious scheme was concocted.

Since the "freeway" passed through the middle of Randy's house, and since the city was persuaded to pay Randy a rather generous sum, he blithely gave up the family homestead, which needed repairs, was somewhat inconvenient for his purposes, and looked rather ordinary anyhow.

I have only a rough idea what his funds might have been at that time, but he certainly might be supposed to have enough to buy or build whatever a bachelor of his tastes might wish.

We were all a little surprised, however, when he bought Armadale, the former residence of Judge Z. T. Weathercott. People said Randy had lost his mind, because Armadale, built sometime in the 1870s, was an absolute wreck. When Henry and I moved here, the old house had already been empty for many years. The windows had been broken, a part of the roof was gone, and its Third Empire tower looked a little bit drunk.

But there was a certain cachet to Armadale. The old judge and his wife were still spoken of for the elegance of their entertaining. The largest window in the Methodist church was dedicated by Bertha Weathercott to the memory of her husband. The street on which the mansion faced had been put through when the Weathercott farm was subdivided and developed for housing in 1950. It was named for the old mansion. Altogether there was still a resonance to the names Weathercott and Armadale which, I suppose, pleased Randy. In any event, he determined to own Armadale (resurrected) on Armadale Drive.

Resurrected the place had to be. The old house was far past restoration. Randy lost no time in having the building pulled down to its stone foundation. An architect friend from Baltimore collaborated with him on the design of a new house, built on the old foundation and therefore incorporating the only usable portion of the judge's old home.

Randy always had a talent for attracting attention to himself, and in that line he was never more successful than he was in the construction of the new Armadale. Loads and loads of river stones were brought in from the Holston. Those who watched its construction said the house would have no resale value at all. But a more detailed description of Randy's new residence will have to wait until later.

At no point did I have much contact with Randy. Oh, to be sure, we met here and there as all who live in towns like Borderville do; and we exchanged chitchat about performances—Randy was always preparing for one. So far as I know, the only times he ever heard me play were on a few instances when he attended midnight mass on Christmas Eve.

I recall meeting him in the bank one day about the time his house was finished. He was full of excitement.

"I'm getting a Bösendorfer concert grand," he said.

A Bösendorfer is to a Baldwin what a Rolls is to an Oldsmobile. A concert grand is to a parlor grand what a stretch limousine is to a Ford Escort.

"Lucky you!" I said, nonplussed.

"Yes," he continued. "With the new house I thought I should get just what I want. If you put that sort of thing off, you know, it never comes to you."

True enough! I, at least, will never have a Bösendorfer concert grand.

"When the house is ready, I am going to give a big party and 'christen' the Bösendorfer."

In about two months he actually did put on a tremendous cocktail party. Henry and I were invited. I went, though Henry had to attend a meeting of the library board that evening.

The Bösendorfer itself was stunning. Randy played Chopin's *Fantasie Impromptu,* the "Prélude" to *Pour le Piano,* and, oh yes, Liszt's *Liebestraum,* which was the only thing most of the guests could recognize.

I say he played these things—he made a dash at them; and the party was a great success.

What did Borderville think of Randy by this time? There were all kinds of opinions: He was a flash in the pan. No, he was not; he was a genius. Yes, he was a genius, but he would never amount to anything. He was gay. He was not gay but dedicated to his art. He was the Renaissance man his mother had talked about so much. There were the pros and cons.

But most of our people can put two and two together and get something that approximates four. I believe that was essentially the process used by little Mrs. Vogelsang when after that Sunday service she reminded me that Randol Hartwell had played for Mrs. Chamberlain's "musical teas." Little old ladies have time to sit around and think about these matters. They like to sort things out and fit them into a pattern, which was why I was inclined to take her seriously.

So I went again to Mrs. Dugan, the housekeeper who had been with Mrs. Chamberlain so long.

"Tell me about Mrs. Chamberlain's doors," I said. "Did she generally keep them locked?"

"Yes, indeed," she answered. "Even in the daytime. It is such a big house, you know. And it would be easy for someone to slip in and neither of us the wiser. Her doors were always locked."

"And the key?" I asked. "Wasn't it inconvenient to get the key every time someone came to the door?"

"No—not at all. You see, we kept the key in the lock."

As anyone would expect!

And there you have it. Randy could have come to "try out the piano," which would have been very natural. He would have practiced while the household went about its business. Then, during a brief pause, it would take less than a minute to make an impression from which to make a key—just for future reference.

I admit that the theory was farfetched, but ultimately it turned out that Mrs. Vogelsang had been right.

A Nugget of Evidence

ROBERT KELSEY

It was about nine-twenty when my wife, Leota, came into the den and said, "If you want hot biscuits tomorrow morning, you had better go to the 7-Eleven. I'm out of biscuit mix."

From our house to the 7-Eleven is only three blocks and a little—far enough for a pleasant walk. In fact, walking there and back is just about all the exercise I take—most days.

The route I take starts at our back door, crosses the backyard, runs down the alley about thirty yards, and then cuts through the vacant lot to Armadale Drive. Then it is north on Armadale to the 7-Eleven.

It's wooded along there, and at night I need a flashlight to cross the vacant lot. But from that point on there is a sidewalk, and the street lights do just fine.

Now you need to know that one block north on Armadale is where Randy Hartwell built his famous house after his mother died. He made quite a noise about it. Got his architect from somewhere way off. That bird was just about a match for Randy himself; and when they got the house finished, it didn't look like anything folks around here had ever seen.

Oh, it was grand all right—sort of spread out in an unusual way. There's a swimming pool, too. It's at the side of the house, but the house doesn't exactly face the street. The fact is, it would be hard to tell where that house faces. Anyhow, old Randy wanted his grounds to be really private. So he planted this hemlock hedge around the place. It's eight or nine feet high now, and he kept it trimmed as neat as could be. The fact is he was just an old maid about a good many things.

What I'm getting at is that as I was about to come to the edge of Randy's property, an old beat-up station wagon turned into his place.

I said to myself, "Hello, something is going on here that won't square with the compass." So I thought, I'll just take a closer look.

The trees are tall on that lot—tall all through there, as a matter of fact. Some of those trees have been there more than a hundred years. So it was dark in those shadows, and I could walk right into the carport and not likely be seen at all.

I got to where the drive goes into the property in time to see the taillights on that station wagon go off. The fellow had pulled into the carport by the side of that little foreign car Randy had. It's right at the kitchen door.

Now you understand all of this happened just a week after they found Randy with that knife stuck into him. Of course right away the police came out and strung that yellow tape they use to keep people off what they call the "crime scene." They were going in and out for two or three days with their investigation, and then they took the tape down.

But still there wasn't any reason for this station wagon to be there. I was pretty sure the police would want to know about a prowler at Randy's house. Most likely this was just a burglar. But again it might have something to do with who killed Randy Hartwell.

Anyhow, I saw right away that it ought to be reported. And to do that, I wanted to have the license number of the station wagon—it was a beat-up old Ford, gray with a lot of rust.

All right then, I went up to the carport. The kitchen door was open, and I could hear the fellow walking around inside. He was using a flashlight.

Well, the fellow in there had no idea that I was on the place. So I turned on my flash and got the license number. It was URK-7295. I was careful to memorize it.

Then I just flashed my light in the back of the wagon there and was about to leave, when something shiny caught my eye.

It's funny sometimes how things come together. If it had been daylight, I probably would not have seen that glint of gold at all. But my flashlight just picked it up right away. And I wanted to know what it was.

As quiet as I could, I opened the back door of that wagon, and there in the folds of an old quilt was this pretty good chunk of gold stuff that looked like it might be part of the frame on that picture of King Louis-Philippe.

I tell you, that just made a thrill run up my spine! Maybe we were going to get our million-dollar picture back.

I latched on to that lump of gold carving and got on down to the 7-Eleven mighty quick to put in a call to the police. By the time I bought my biscuit mix and the new *Hunter and Fisher* magazine, the squad car was there and the officers were in the house.

I figured everything was in good hands, so I went on home to see if I could fit that chunk of plaster into our frame.

It fitted exactly.

I called Mrs. Delaporte right away. Seeing that she was president of the Historical Society, I thought she ought to know what I had found. I asked her whether she wanted me to notify the police about the chunk of gold carved stuff or did she prefer to do it herself.

She kind of paused a bit and then said, "We don't want that piece of the molding to get lost. It might be better to wait until morning and take it to the chief of police himself."

Well, that made sense, because that little chunk of gold was the first and only clue that might lead us to our million-dollar painting.

So as soon as I got off the phone, I went back down to the Hartwell place to make sure that the police got their man. I came on to Armadale Drive just in time to see the squad car take off for town. I figured they must be taking that fellow to jail. I went on down to the house, and sure enough, the old station wagon was still there and the house was locked and empty.

I don't mind telling you I was just as excited as a kid on the night before Christmas. But that didn't keep me from sleeping. I generally do that pretty well.

New Light on Our Problem

ROBERT KELSEY

I've known Police Chief Runnels since way back. He's a heavyset fellow with sandy hair—good, steady sort. Soon as he saw me through his open door that next morning, he said, "Bob Kelsey, come in this office."

Of course we talked a little about different things before I got down to business and asked him if our intruder was still in jail.

"That was a false alarm," he said. "The boys brought the fellow here to the station and interrogated him. But they had to let him go."

I guess my face said what I had in mind, because Runnels laughed.

"Your burglar turned out to be Randy's nephew."

When I still didn't say anything, he went on: "Like the new owner, you might say. And besides, he told the desk sergeant he was in the house to pick up a pair of swimming trunks he had left there. He even had the trunks to show for it."

But in my pocket I had that chunk from the frame of Louis's portrait. And no matter how much right Spud Shankley might have to come and go at that house, I saw no reason why our frame and maybe our picture had any business at all of being in Spud's station wagon—any time for any reason.

I put my hand in my pocket and was about to show the chief what I had there.

Then I adjusted my whole way of looking at the matter—did it in a mighty short time, too.

You see, the evidence in my pocket was going to get Spud Shankley into trouble, and aside from the fact that he was some kind of relative of my wife. . . . Well, you see how that was. The least I could do would be to talk to Spud before I said anything more to the police.

I apologized to the chief for causing trouble. He said I had done the right thing to report what he called "the incident," and I left like a cur dog with his tail between his legs.

The more I thought about it on the way home, the more it seemed to me that our fine Mr. Spud Shankley owed us a mighty clear explanation of how part of the frame of a million-dollar painting got into his station wagon.

When I finally got hold of Spud on the phone, I said, "Son, you're in trouble."

"What did I do?"

I said, "You know as well as I do that you weren't looking for any swimming trunks when the police hauled you out of Randy's house and took you down to the station. You were looking for something more like a million dollars' worth of picture."

That stumped him.

"Look," he said, "I never done nothing wrong."

"We'll just see about that." I was pretty stern with him. "You get yourself over here to my house mighty quick, or I'll have the police on you for stealing property belonging to the Historical Society of Ambrose County."

In about ten minutes here he came.

"I never stole nothing," he commenced even before I opened the screen door.

I didn't have a bit of trouble getting him to talk. It just came rolling out of him. He spilled the whole thing down to the least detail. Randy had offered him fifty dollars in return for a little hauling in that station wagon of his—said that he, Randy, was doing some restoration work on the painting for Mrs. Chamberlain.

This claim didn't seem at all fishy to Spud—seeing that Randy was always doing strange things like that anyhow. Randy was kind of a Jack-of-all-trades when it came to art and such. Spud's grandmother kept Spud on a short leash for money. And after all, it was his uncle—great-uncle really—who made him the offer. And though Randy might seem a strange hero for a harum-scarum teenager like Spud, you must remember that Randy as a relative would have to look a whole lot better than Margie, the boy's sour-faced grandma. Randy was rich—or seemed so—smooth as the devil himself, handsome as a movie star. And then on the other side was Margie, sharp-tongued old Margie in her greasy apron. Randy might be a queer or not a queer, but that kind of thing doesn't call for horror in the young today like it did in my time.

And then, of course, Randy had Mrs. Chamberlain's key—proof, you understand, that the job was all right. Randy had explained that Mrs. Chamberlain was in the hospital, which meant that the time was ideal for the project since it would not discommode the lady in the least.

Spud had thought it a little strange that Randy required him to wear gloves during their expedition, but Randy said they had to use the gloves to protect the gilt frame from fingerprints that would tarnish it. Spud suspected nothing. But he never did understand why Randy wanted to carry out the activity at two o'clock in the morning.

"Do you want the fifty dollars?" Randy had said.

Does the mouse want cheese? Of course Spud wanted fifty dollars. And so the time was agreed upon—an hour which required Spud to sneak out to the house and would ensure that he would keep the whole episode from Margie.

Spud explained that they had gone into the alley behind 902 Chestnut Street. Using Randy's key, they had entered the house through the back door, removed the painting from the landing, carried it out to Spud's wreck of a station wagon, wrapped it very carefully in the old quilt, and thus hauled it to Randy's house. There the picture had been taken to the cellar.

"I'll be working on this for about an hour," Randy said. "You go upstairs and watch TV."

Since there were adult channels, not of the homosexual kind, to be watched on Randy's TV, Spud was not at all opposed to the suggestion.

The restoration of oil paintings being a subject that had never crossed Spud's empty mind, he raised no question about what had gone on in the basement. An hour later, it did not seem to bother him that the picture looked exactly the same as it had before. And the fact that they returned it to its original place above the landing of Mrs. Chamberlain's stair was reassurance to Spud that nothing illegal had been done, though he did wonder why they had to keep gloves on until they were out of the house.

Randy told his nephew that the treatment he had given the painting would have to be repeated and there would be a further fifty-dollar payment if Spud was available at that time.

About a month later the two of them went through the whole process exactly as it had been performed before. Again, any notion that something illegal might have been done was erased by the fact of the return of King Louis's portrait to its place above that landing.

"And so," I said, "you had no notion that you had done anything that the police would question?"

"No, no," he protested—injured to his soul that I had even thought such a thing.

"Then explain," I demanded, "your presence in your uncle's house last night when the police came."

He was looking for his swimming trunks. He had told the police all about it at the station; and when they knew that he was nephew and next of kin to the deceased householder, and that he had got into the house with a key that Randy, the late householder, had given him the previous January in order that Spud could water certain house plants while Randy was away for a week—when the police had satisfied themselves of all this, and when he had shown them the swim trunks he was supposed to have come to look for, they had brought him back to the house on Armadale Drive, where Spud had gotten into his wagon and gone home to his grandmother's house, being at pains not to waken her.

"Spud," I said, fixing him firmly with my eye, "weren't you in that house looking for the *real* portrait of Louis-Philippe which you had read in the paper is worth one million dollars?"

"Oh no, no," he protested.

But he knew that I knew what he had been up to. And he knew that I knew that he knew I knew.

Sort that out any way you want to, I now had the upper hand over Spud Shankley. He was ready to do anything I told him to do.

I tried to call Mrs. Delaporte, but when I couldn't get her, I called Henry Delaporte instead.

Certain Legal Matters Are Arranged

HENRY DELAPORTE

My conversation with Bob Kelsey was of considerable interest. I already knew from the telephone consultation he had held with my wife on the previous evening that he had found the evidence of the gesso chipped from the frame of Louis's portrait. Consequently, I was forced to acknowledge that Helen's friend Mrs. Vogelsang had been right and that Randy had masterminded an ingenious substitution of a forgery for the very valuable painting that had been willed to the Historical Society.

Aware that Helen would want to be immediately cognizant of even the slightest information related to the theft, I called the parish office at Saint Luke's and prevailed upon the church secretary to inform Helen, who was at the organ practicing, that I would apprise her of certain developments if she would have a cup of coffee and a slice of cheesecake with me at KP Duty, a small but excellent restaurant that we have here on Division Street.

We sat at a sidewalk table and discussed the newest developments. There was no need to lower our voices; information of the kind that we were discussing would be bruited to the whole town in spite of any precautions to the contrary.

After we had discussed the possible ramifications of the situation for a pleasant half hour, Helen said triumphantly, "I told you Frances Vogelsang would be right about it." She was reminding me that woman's intuition had been tested and proved true.

"But do we know this Spud Shankley?" she asked.

From the tenor of Bob Kelsey's remarks about Spud's grandmother, I had gathered that Margie Hartwell was not likely to be within Helen's circle of acquaintance. Spud himself, however, was destined to become decidedly well known to us.

In fact, I got to know him when I returned to the office and found the young man sitting alongside Bob Kelsey in our waiting room—early for the appointment Bob and I had set up.

At Bob's prompting, Spud told me substantially the story contained in the chapter preceding this one.

When I had heard the full account, I put the question to the boy: "Were you in fact looking for the painting when the police found you?"

Spud looked sheepishly at Bob, who, in a rather severe voice said, "Tell the truth."

And of course he had been looking for the picture, as anyone with his knowledge of the affair would have done.

"Did you find it?"

"No."

"Why did you think the picture was in the house?" I asked.

"I knew it was there because it was too big to go in Randy's Alfa Romeo."

It was a good answer. The boy had figured it out. And of course the limitation of Randy Hartwell's transportive facilities lay at the root of Spud's involvement in the affair in the first place. I believed the boy, and I thought we had enough to protect him from immediate arrest when we laid all of this before the authorities, which, of course, we would have to do.

I put one more question.

"Do you know who made the forged copy of the portrait?"

I could tell from Spud's face that the question was crossing his mind for the first time. It is amazing how long the tabula rasa remains unsullied on what passes for the mind of the young.

At this point, at Bob's suggestion, we came to a formal agreement that I should be retained to represent Spud's interest in the estate, as well as any matters which might involve him with the police. Bob is a hardheaded, shrewd sort of fellow. He was of course putting me in a position to look for clues to Randy's activities relating to the theft of the painting, as well as giving me an advantageous position to safeguard it should it be found.

We went from my office to the city justice center, where Spud made full disclosure. Chief Runnels was at a loss to know what charge to make. Although, as I learned later, Spud had been questioned immediately after the discovery of Randy's death and questioned again after being discovered at Randy's house as the result of Bob's complaint, the boy's involvement in the removal of the painting from the Chamberlain property was news to Runnels. He said he had never had previous experience of a voluntary confession of breaking and entry in a case where the police had not been called.

I pointed out that there had actually been no breaking in on Spud's part, inasmuch as the door had been opened by a key and that my client had acted under the impression that Randy Hartwell was removing the portrait on Mrs. Chamberlain's instruction. The means by which Hartwell had secured the key were unknown to my client, and consequently the most severe charge that could be brought was trespassing.

Chief Runnels agreed, registered a formal charge, and released Spud to Bob's custody.

I then guided my client to the Probate Clerk of the Chancery Court, where we began dealing with the estate of Randol Hartwell, deceased. A few days later when the matter came before the judge, he took a speculative look at Spud.

"Next of kin, you say?"

Spud nodded.

"Is there an older person in your family who might be appointed administrator?"

The wheels whirred rapidly in Spud's head as he undoubtedly envisioned his grandmother in that position. A look of dismay came over his face.

"No," he said faintly. Then thinking better of it, he said, "Mr. Kelsey."

Judge Meath looked at Kelsey and said, "Bob, do you know anything about administering estates?"

"Well, I administered my mother's estate back in seventy-eight."

"I remember your mother," the judge observed. "I must warn you the estate of Randol Hartwell is likely to be quite another matter." It was certainly true that Bob's mother's estate was by no means comparable to Randy's.

The judge looked absently out the window. He turned again and said, "Bob, this estate will be too much for you to handle. I am therefore going to do something a little irregular. Henry, if you have no objection, I think I'll appoint you administrator."

And that is how I became very intimately involved in the tangled affairs of the late Randol Hartwell.

Randol's Dream House

HELEN DELAPORTE

The first thing I said when Henry told me the news that he was to administer the Hartwell estate was, "Let's go look for the picture." I had no doubt that we would find it, perhaps ingeniously hidden, somewhere in Randy's house.

And so, dinner had no sooner been finished than we went over to Armadale Drive.

Though I had been there before, I didn't remember it at all clearly, and what I remembered only made me curious to see what I had not seen before.

The orientation of the present house, built as it is upon the foundation of the former mansion, is quite strange—the side, rather than the front, being toward the street.

The result is a decidedly odd approach to a very pretentious house. One comes to it through the gap in a thick hemlock hedge and arrives—of all things—at a carport with immediate access to the kitchen door.

Of course we could have taken the flagstone walk to the right, around the corner of the house, and so to the official "front" door. But under present circumstances there was no need for that.

As it was, when Henry turned the key and opened the door, we found the kitchen in unholy disorder.

"Something will have to be done about this," I said. There were dirty dishes, empty beer and vodka bottles, glasses, and paper napkins piled about.

"Obviously a party on the night of the murder," Henry observed. He counted the plates. "Ten people," he concluded.

"Well, they certainly made a mess," I said.

"Maybe the distaff side of this administration could figure out how to take care of it," Henry mumbled. Under other circumstances, I would have told him that the problem was his, but since he was really taking on this business because of me and my interest in the stolen painting, I merely made a mental note to find out who "did" for Randy and have her clean up the mess.

From the kitchen, we went into the dining room. The walls there are burnt orange. The room is not really large enough to accommodate the French provincial table and eight highly carved oak chairs with caned backs. There is a tremendous crystal chandelier—decidedly excessive, but it made its point. At what may be considered the end of the room is an ornate sideboard of roughly the same period as the chairs. Between two heavily draped windows on the long side of the room stood a heavy credenza.

"Aha!" I said.

"Yes?" Henry's mind was not where mine was.

"Could our picture be behind that?"

"The picture?"

"Yes—behind the credenza!"

"The credenza isn't tall enough."

"But if the picture were on its side," I suggested.

"It still wouldn't work."

Although I leaned my head against the wall and squinted, it was too dark behind that heavy chest to see anything. But by running my hand as far as I could into the space between the credenza and the wall, I was soon convinced that our picture could not possibly be there.

The next room was the living room, the only room, aside from a guest bathroom, with which I was familiar. It is very impressive. I would guess it might measure forty feet by thirty, and it just goes up and up. Henry observed that it might do very well for a basketball court.

The walls are blue. The floors are parquet. The first thing I noticed was the horrid stain on the Bokhara rug at my feet.

"That's where Randy was killed," I said, pointing to the spot.

"No doubt," Henry replied.

"What a lot of blood," I observed. "It's spooky!"

"If you are going to deal with murder," Henry replied, "you have to expect blood."

As usual, he was right. This was the third time I had been involved in "dealing" with murder. This time, however, I was looking at the dried blood of someone I had actually known. I found it very spooky.

"Tomorrow morning, the first thing you do as administrator is to send that rug to be cleaned," I ordered, and Henry made the sound that I had learned to interpret as absentminded agreement.

But to describe the living room:

It is typical of Randy's ostentation, and in spite of its eccentricities, it comes off remarkably well. At least as large as two normal rooms, the far end is dominated conventionally enough by a fireplace. The other end is a kind of shrine to Randy's musical pursuits, featuring a stage, perhaps a foot or so high, on which stands his Bösendorfer concert grand.

While half of the furniture is arranged to face the fireplace, the other half faces the Bösendorfer.

The dividing axis of the room is further indicated by a gorgeous Oriental runner more or less indicating a path from the front door in the middle of the south wall to French doors in the middle of the north wall. The front door looks out onto a flagstone deck, while the French doors open to Randy's swimming pool.

Exactly in the middle of the room stands an art moderne table boasting a plate-glass top supported by brass legs. Immediately above hangs a very grand chandelier in the same style.

All rugs—placed here and there—are Oriental. All chairs and sofas, with the exception of two high-backed eighteenth-century wing chairs in floral tapestry, are luxuriously upholstered in white velvet.

The furniture along the walls particularly interested us because we felt sure that our painting, if hidden in this or any other room, would have been placed behind some large chest or similar item. In this room, decorated as it was in the modern manner, the prospect of finding our portrait did not seem very promising. I shall, however, describe our search.

To the left as we entered the room there was a grandfather's clock, silent since Randy's death, when it was not rewound. Flanking the French doors were console tables similar to the glass-topped table in the center of the room. Above these consoles hung two of Randy's nonobjective canvases—rather effective as decorative features.

Near one corner of the east wall was a door opening on a hall about which I shall say something later. Between this door and a centrally situated fireplace there was a bookcase enclosed in an arched recess. Another like it appeared on the other side of the fireplace. They held Randy's books—many of them dealing with art and furniture—handsome volumes featuring excellent reproductions.

Do not think that the presence of impressive bookcases is any indication that Randy was an assiduous reader. Almost half the space was taken up with various decorative objects—vases, omari plates, figurines, that sort of thing. The books that did not deal with art or interior design tended to be standard sets—Conrad, Bret Hart, Emerson, and *The World Book Encyclopedia*.

The bookcases seemed firmly attached to their alcoves and were an architectural feature. I did not see how Randy could hide anything behind them without seriously defacing the woodwork. Our attention was next drawn to the fireplace.

Over the mantel we observed another large painting. It too was nonobjective, containing shapes that clearly had been inspired by the piano—something that could very well have been the pedal lyre, somewhat warped, of course; a part of the music stand; and four-inch black-and-white alternating stripes cascading in an S-curve perhaps intended to suggest piano keys forming an arpeggio. It was not Randy's work, but signed by E.S. And, alas, it was not large enough for Louis-Philippe to be lurking behind it.

The remainder of the east wall was taken up by a door that opened onto a guest bedroom, in which we found a four-poster bed with chintz curtains and a deep flounce. The bed was unmade and was obviously the one that had been occupied by the unknown guest on the night of the murder, as reported by the *Banner-Democrat*. Aha, I thought, perhaps our painting is under the bed; but it wasn't. I noted that the room had obviously been thoroughly dusted for fingerprints.

We searched the closet and the bath next door, which also served as a second guest room.

Returning to the living room, we observed that the south

wall with its four windows offered no place at all for concealment.

The southwest corner of the room, as I have explained, featured the stage, reached by two steps, on which Randy displayed his vaunted concert grand, draped with a heavily fringed Spanish shawl. On it he had placed a large free-form vase. It was glazed in lavender and brown with a touch of turquoise, no doubt the work of Sprote, a local ceramicist. Behind the piano was a large three-panel screen, painted, again in the nonobjective manner, by Randy. I looked behind that screen, but our picture was not there.

To Henry I put the question: "Do you have any idea how much a piano of that size and quality costs these days?"

It was purely rhetorical. Not in a thousand years would Henry have guessed.

"Around seventy-five thousand," I said. Henry looked quite surprised.

We were now satisfied that our painting could not have been hidden in the living room. We went therefore into Randy's bedroom.

This room is reached directly from the stage—to allow him, I suppose, to step directly to the piano if the mood struck him during the night, perhaps to play the Moonlight Sonata! Yes, I am being snide and catty.

Randy's bedroom is a bit larger than those assigned to guests. It had to be so in order to accommodate a king-sized waterbed—unmade, the covers thrown back probably when Randy had gotten up on that fatal night and walked to his death through the door by which we had just entered.

Apart from the disorder of the bedclothes, the room was in apple-pie order.

"When the girl comes to do the dishes," I said, "I'll have her take care of the beds, too."

"What difference does it make?" Henry asked. "No one is going to sleep in them."

It was one of those sex differences that are not supposed to exist. And yet, it was not altogether my housekeeping instinct. I am not afraid of the dead or of death itself. If you have read *The Famous DAR Murder Mystery,* you may remember that I examined the corpse of Mr. García in some detail without the slightest shudder. But there was something about Randy's house so filled with the personality of its recent owner, the unfinished business in the kitchen, the clock that had run down, the blood on the rug, and now the unmade beds—something that two weeks after the event projected a most unpleasant sensation.

There was Randy's writing desk, and in one corner of his room, a large "entertainment center." We looked behind it. We also looked in the closet and in the bathroom. There was nothing to be found!

Since a waterbed rests directly on the floor, there could be nothing hidden under it. And so there was no place in the vicinity of Randy's more private digs to hide what we were seeking.

Having now searched the kitchen, dining room, living room, one guest room, Randy's bedroom, Randy's closet, and Randy's bath, we made our way to the hall leading to the second guest room, the study, and the cellar stairs. In doing so, we crossed the living room diagonally, and thus our attention was attracted more specifically by the glass table in the middle of the room.

There between alabaster bookends were two handsomely bound volumes. The title of one was *Carnelian and Gold.* It proved to contain poems by Randy himself. The other was *Rustlings of the Spirit,* the work of Erindell Schovall, a lady poet from Deedsville, a small town some fifty miles from Borderville. I paused, opened first one volume and then the other, and discovered that both were printed in Italy, at the poets' expense, no doubt. That the two should have been isolated in such obvious "togetherness" raised Henry's eyebrows. And I agreed with him, but more about that later.

Passing through the doorway, we observed ahead of us the stairs to the basement. There were doors to the right and to the left. The door to the right opened on the second bedroom, which, as I have noted, shared the bath with the other guest room.

When we were satisfied that there was no hidden painting in this room, we crossed the hall and stepped through the door on the opposite side. Here we found a very pleasant room that seemed to be a study. The east wall had a grand fireplace with a marble mantel, above which hung a large and very dark painting, but not the one I was seeking. Between the two windows on the north side stood a magnificent eighteenth-century secretary-bookcase, elaborately ornamented with inlay. I could not see behind it because the window facings framed it so closely. It was a place where a large painting that, after all, had been removed from its frame could have been hidden. Fortunately, the secretary was on casters.

Henry saw the look in my eye.

"Do you want me to move it out?" he offered.

"If you can," I said.

He braced one knee against the wall and, with a groan, heaved manfully. The secretary moved about five inches. There was nothing behind it but cobwebs.

The window in the other wall looked out onto a very attractive pool of oval shape, enclosed by a brick wall about seven feet high. I would say that Randy had a thing about privacy. Poolside beach chairs and a chaise-longue were draped here and there with discarded towels.

"It must have been quite a party," I said. "It looks as though they had a cook-out here by the pool."

"There's something I don't get," Henry said. "This big house, the fancy furniture, the pool—all for one lone man! There is a restless pursuit here, but for what?"

Randy's lifestyle did indeed seem to be a pursuit but without cohesion—without consistent aim.

So much for the study. And now for the basement.

Like any cellar, it contained items "too numerous to mention." But I will mention just a few.

There was of course the obligatory furnace. Randy used gas. There was also a laundry room. There was what would have to be called a studio, which appeared to be used not only for painting but also for photography, because Randy had a darkroom next to it. There were shelves and cupboards, some flower pots, boxes neatly stacked, a number of canvases painted upon and some not yet painted upon, and steel filing cabinets.

This was an omnium gatherum that would have to be investigated at length, but we agreed to put that off until another day.

I hand it to Randy: He was neat in his habits. At least that conglomerate of things that had been necessary or useful once—things that most of us cannot make up our minds about when it comes to having them around—were stored in perfect order but kept underground so that everything upstairs might seem serene.

The same principle seems to have been characteristic of Randy in other ways as well. There was so much under the surface—so much that we didn't see.

In Search of the Guests

ROBERT KELSEY

When Mrs. Delaporte told me there had been a party at Randy Hartwell's house the night he was killed and that the dirty dishes were still in the kitchen, I thought I just might try to find answers to a few questions.

We knew that Randy had stolen our picture and how he had done it. Where was it now?

We didn't know, but Spud thought it was at the house—Randy's, that is—because Spud had last seen it there and was looking for it when the police caught him at it and I found that chunk that fell out of the frame. It stood to reason that our picture was still at Randy's unless Randy had found some means other than Spud's old station wagon to take it where he was going to sell it or maybe put it up for auction.

Now, how could he move something as big as that? UPS wouldn't take a package that size, and Randy would have to sign the slip and declare the value if he shipped it by one of the freight lines.

And even if he got a freight line to handle it, one thing sent by itself has to ride along with kitchen stoves, baby beds, spading forks, and all the rest of the things folks send along when they are transferred. And if there's stuff from several families aboard one of those eighteen-wheelers, it may take damn near a month before your one item gets where it's going.

And think of the kind of damage that could happen to the picture in that time. Then there would be the insurance, and if the word go out—the way it did—about Louis's portrait, worth a million dollars, being stolen, well, you know that anybody in Borderville who had handled a box that big and that shape would remember and make up his mind in two minutes to turn in Randy for the reward.

So I didn't think that picture waltzed out of Randy's house in any freight truck.

Could Randy have rolled up the canvas and put it in a mailing tube? If the paint on the real picture was as thick as the paint on the copy, it would crack all to pieces. And there's no point in stealing a picture if it's going to be in such a shape that you can't sell it.

But there could be somebody else with a van or station wagon that Randy could use. I thought about that a good while and wasn't especially happy about the idea.

In the first place, by the time the move was made, it was beans to doughnuts the fellow helping Randy would be onto what was happening. Why, even Spud figured it out after a while. Not that the fact that Randy stole the picture would stop a fellow from moving the picture for Randy. No, he would just want his part of that million dollars.

Now, the rumor going around town for a long time was that Randy was queer. Whether he was queer meaning odd or the other kind, I don't have what you would call evidence—though I do state that he definitely was not like the rest of the folks in these parts. Anyhow, people are saying—because Randy was naked when the body was found—that the police think it was a homosexual lover who killed him.

Being no expert on the subject, I can only speculate that the police jumped at the idea some lover was jealous or angry and fixed old Randy by putting that fancy knife between his ribs.

But here's another maybe. Maybe this homosexual lover knew about the picture—maybe Randy told him about it the way straight men sometimes tell their wives something and later wish they hadn't. And then maybe this homosexual lover wanted his part of the million dollars and Randy said no. I bet that would put an end to the love affair right quick.

I didn't expect to solve this mystery right away. After all, it wouldn't *be* a mystery if folks could see through it right from the beginning. But there was one thing at least that I could do. And so I did it. I phoned every freight line in the book and asked if Randy Hartwell had been shipping any boxes or packages a little over three foot wide by six foot long by six inches thick. And those fellows—fellows and two young ladies—knew me because of all those years when I worked at the post office, and they didn't mind giving me the information. And pretty soon I knew that Randy hadn't sent off any picture by truck.

I called U-Haul, too, but the picture hadn't gone that route either. And I didn't think Randy would try to move it on the top of that Alfa Romeo—no, sir. Too public, don't you see?

And that threw me back to wondering if after all it had been a friend with a van or an RV that had helped Randy move the thing; and then it popped into my mind that Randy could ask for the use of the RV or van just to borrow and say he was moving something else—like a table or a sofa. But surely that would have sounded mighty fishy because Randy would have to have somebody help him load something big like that. Still, he could say, "I'll come by and pick up your van," and then add, "I have this fellow that's going to help me load up."

So I was right back where I started. But the pure truth is that I just didn't see how that picture could be in the house, where the police didn't find it when they investigated and Spud didn't find it. And Mrs. Delaporte and Henry didn't find it. And I didn't see how Randy could have moved it out of the house, though one or t'other must have been the case.

Now, the person that had been in the house when Randy was killed had slept in the guest room. That didn't sound much like a lover, did it? So what would cause the fellow in the guest room to get up in the middle of the night and kill Randy? Maybe this guest was stealing our picture, and Randy came out of his room to object, and the other fellow killed Randy and made off with Louis-Philippe.

If he was a guest, he must have been a friend, or at least Randy must have thought he was a friend. And he would have to know Randy pretty well if he knew about the picture. And if so, was he at the party that night? Was he from out of town? And if he—or maybe she—was not from out of town, what was the point of spending the night at Randy's house but not in bed with Randy?

To bring all this together, I decided to find out about the nine guests who were at the party.

It took three tries before I could get young Spud on the phone.

"Hey, young man," I said, "I'm supposed to be responsible for you and I haven't seen you in two days."

He made a little old excuse about how he had had to do something for his grandma.

"Now, look," I said, "I've done some pretty big favors for you. If it wasn't for me, you could be in jail. It's time for you to do something for me."

Silence at the other end of the line.

"Are you there?"

"Yeah."

It was 9:30 P.M.

"What do you say I buy you a pizza?" I had the impression that at nineteen my wife's airhead cousin might still be a bottomless pit.

"You buying?"

"That's what I said."

With that, the deal was made. I would meet him in fifteen minutes at Pizza Joe's. It would be noisy—very noisy—but I could buy pizza for him and decaf for me. And possibly by the time the pizza was gone, I would know what I needed to know.

After we had ordered our stuff, I guided Spud to a corner table as far from the music as possible.

"I need some information," I said.

He looked at me as if I was a tiresome old goat of an adult, like his grandma.

"Well, what's wrong with that?" I said in answer to his sullen stare.

"Nothin'."

"Spud," I said, "I need to know something about Randy's friends, and you're about the only one that can tell me."

"You mean like what the police asked."

I judged he meant the interrogation that was held right after the murder. Yes, I wanted to know that much and maybe more.

"Well, Randy had this party, see?" the boy began.

"That's the night Randy was killed?"

"Yeah."

"Were you there?"

"Yeah, me and Kay. She's my steady."

"Your steady? What's the matter you don't have a date tonight?"

"Her old lady put her in solitary because we honky-tonked last Saturday and her mom woke up when Kay got home at four-thirty."

This information made me wonder whether it was such a bad thing that Leota and I never had children. But I got back to the object of our little get-together.

"You were at the party with Kay," I said. "How long did you stay?"

"We went there in the afternoon about three to swim. Pretty soon Randy's gang began to come in, and he started passing out the good stuff about four."

"Good stuff? Would you be a little more specific?"

"You know, beer."

"Nothing but beer?" You see, I thought "good stuff" probably meant something else.

"Oh, there was vodka and lots of other stuff, but Kay only likes beer. Well, I had these tickets to Jellyfish Salad in Parsons City, so Randy put a couple of steaks on for us about five-thirty."

I judged correctly that Jellyfish Salad was a rock group.

"Who else was at the party?" I asked. I was beginning to be afraid Spud might not have been there long enough to have helpful information.

"All right," he said, "there was me and Kay and Charlie Gunn."

I've known Charlie Gunn for twenty years or more. He is a florist—small fellow, on the quiet side. I didn't know, however, that he was a friend of Randy's. But come to think of it, there were similarities. Charlie's mother, Mrs. Gunn, was like Nettie Marie Hartwell, a widow who no doubt doted on an only son. What Nettie Marie had been to furniture in Borderville, Mrs. Gunn had been to flowers. I had heard that she was bedridden now, and Charlie ran the shop by himself.

I wrote down "Charlie Gunn" on a small pad I had brought along. With Spud, Kay, and Randy, that made four.

"Who else?"

"Tommie Torrence and Billy Ray Holder. They are hooked up."

"Hooked up?"

"You know—fags living together."

Well, if that is what it was, I supposed that was the easiest way to say it. I wrote down "Tommie Torrence," but as I began to write "Billy Ray Holder," I suddenly realized that the name was actually William Raymond Holder, a loan officer at the Volunteer Bank and Trust.

"And you're sure they are hooked up."

"Oh, yeah. But def."

I took "def" to mean that Spud was certain about it. I wrote "hooked up" after the names. But I did not know who Torrence was. So I put the question.

"Oh, he's a chiphead somewhere."

"Chiphead?"

"You know. Like, computers all the time."

"All right. Who else was there?"

It went like that through the entire list of them, but Spud knew all the guests that were there that night, and in a way he knew something about each of them. His observations were those of a nineteen-year-old. But I hand it to him: the boy seemed to know what he was talking about.

There were glimmers of intelligence in my wife's young cousin. If only he had learned something useful in those nineteen years! With that grandmother of his, it must have been hell at home. And equally it would have been a relief to escape to Randy's place, where the world was full of sunshine and everyone would be accommodating. I didn't get the idea that Spud was likely to pick up anything very useful from contact with Randy.

At any rate, I got the list, and an odd one it is:

    Spud
    Kay
    Charles Gunn (the florist)
    Tommie Torrence (computer operator)
    Wm. R. Holder (Volunteer Bank)
    Ted Grigsley (Clerk at gas company)—called
        The Grig
    Tony Braun (runs a gym)
    Maybelle Sprote
    Erindell Schovall (woman from Deedsville)
    Randy

It was not all easy sledding, this business of dragging information out of Spud. But if I struck upon just the right question, I found that he had a good deal to say.

He had much to tell about Tony Braun.

Tony is a bodybuilder. At first that really surprised me. That kind of development wasn't at all what I thought would appeal to Randy. But then, I had heard rumors that many bodybuilders were gay. Spud thought this one was a little spacy but not gay.

Tony has The Body Shop, a gym in an old building in an alley off Singleton over on the Virginia side of town. I got the idea that the gym was just a means of support while Tony got himself in shape to compete for titles in the beefcake line. Randy, with his early experience in ballet, was helping Tony with posing—the kind of thing we sometimes see on TV, where a big hunk comes out and ripples his muscles and pumps himself up like a balloon.

According to Spud, Tony spent a good part of his time beside Randy's pool, a deep tan being required in Tony's line of work.

Spud seemed to admire Tony's physical achievement to a degree. He just didn't think it was worth the time and effort Tony had put into it.

Now, about Maybelle Sprote—Spud didn't seem to know much about her. But after a few minutes of discussion, he said something about pots; and I realized this was the woman who makes the high-priced pottery—strange-looking vases and pitchers too small at the top to be of any use, but so wide at the bottom that they take up a lot of space.

Spud dismissed her as "random," which turned out to mean odd. While Randy was supervising the cook-out, Maybelle paired off with Schovall, which was only natural as neither of these ladies, according to Spud, could be expected to be attracted to any male present except, perhaps, Randy.

And then, finally, there was Erindell, who seemed to be past Spud's powers of description. "Spacy" was the only thing he could say about her.

What a strange party that must have been! An obviously normal teenager, Spud, and his girlfriend; a pair of gays—one an officer in the bank and the other a computer operator; a florist who continues a family business that has been in operation on the Virginia side of Borderville as long as anyone cares to remember; a clerk with the gas company; the bodybuilder; and the two women—the fancy potter and Erindell.

Erindell Schovall is noted around here as a poet. We see her name often enough in the *Banner-Democrat*, but she lives in Deedsville, which is almost fifty miles away. I've never read any of her stuff, but it seems that women's clubs have her in once in a while to read to them.

She is connected somehow to the Deeds family, and they have been in this part of Tennessee long enough to think they invented the place. One of them was a judge, and another wanted to be a state senator not long ago. I have never seen the woman, but when the paper runs her picture, it is always the same one, which was taken long enough ago to make me think she is around sixty.

As for Maybelle Sprote, I have seen her in the post office and other places. She is what we used to call plain and doesn't waste time trying to hide it. What's more, she is stout and wears mostly tan or brown, and sandals that look as though she made them herself. In cold weather she never wears a coat, but rather a cape sort of thing about as heavy as a horse blanket.

Although when you think about it, the way she dresses is sensible, all the same I understand why Spud said she was "random." Plain and without makeup, she is no more than forty at the very oldest. But practical as her getup may be, her pots are impractical, and therefore she qualifies as an artist, which makes her a satisfactory match with Erindell Schovall. So those two were probably there to raise the tone of the party.

When I looked at the guest list for the party, I could see only two things that they all had in common: (1) Randy knew them; and (2) they all agreed to come.

But I have got off the track of my story. What I started out to do was find out if any of them had a car that might be used to transport a portrait of Louis-Philippe painted by Charles Willson Peale. Cars are more in the line of Spud's interest, and it turned out that he knew the answers for each of the guests.

Holder and Torrence had come in a BMW—the ordinary model that couldn't possibly accommodate anything as big as the stolen portrait.

The Grig, as Spud called Ted Grigsley, had a Ford Escort, but it was only the sedan, not the station wagon.

Tony Braun came on a bicycle.

Maybelle Sprote came in a pint-sized Isuzu.

The Schovall woman came in a Cadillac suitable to a member of the Deeds family but not big enough for the painting.

So that left little Charlie Gunn, who came in his florist's van. I thought about this for a minute or so and put a line under Charlie's name.

Then I said, "Think hard, Spud. Have you ever seen a delivery truck or van—or station wagon—come to this house in the last month?"

After a moment of thought, Spud shrugged. That was as far as I got with Spud.

Was there really a connection between Randy's death and the disappearance of our picture, after all? And should the Historical Society confine itself to the search for our painting and forget about the murder? But if the two *were* connected, wouldn't the answer to one mystery be the answer to the other?

However that might be, it looked like it was my duty as a member of the Society to turn over any facts I found to Mrs. Delaporte, our president, or to Henry Delaporte, the administrator of the estate, and of course—depending on what it was—to the police.

The Financial Condition of Mr. Randol Hartwell

HENRY DELAPORTE

Upon receiving letters testamentary, I embarked on the inventory of the estate of Randol Paul Hartwell, deceased. As my friend Dick Meath had predicted, the task, which began in the normal way, was soon complicated.

I began, as is customary, at Randy's bank, the Volunteer Bank and Trust Company. Myra Durfey, who presides over the vault there, led me to a box of the smallest size. I would have expected something much larger for the scion of a family at one time quite prominent among the merchants on Division Street. But no larger box was needed for the following articles:

1. A certificate of annuity paying $1,000 per month

2. Title to the property at 1225 Armadale Drive

3. 1,000 shares of preferred stock in the Great Southwestern Virginia & East Tennessee Gas Exploration Company, which may best be described as "inactive," its sole capital being a few mineral leases that did not warrant drilling at the time the company went bankrupt

4. A string of pearls

5. Three diamond rings

6. Title to the family plot in Maplehurst Cemetery

7. $1,600 in cash

This last item immediately suggested to me that Randy had made a practice of fiddling with his income tax reports.

In the same bank there was a checking account containing $382.39.

The reader will no doubt realize from my wife's full and revealing account of Randy's house and his implied lifestyle that some other source of income and perhaps an additional pool of capital would be necessary to keep Randy in operation. It was going to be my task to find out just how that might be. I certainly was not going to find it at the Volunteer Bank.

Accordingly, I went to the house on Armadale Drive and let myself into the kitchen. I was glad to see that my wife had contacted Norella Mae, Randy's black cleaning woman, and that she had put things to rights. I scanned the living room as I passed through, noting that the carpet cleaners had come on the day Norella Mae was there as Helen had arranged for them to and that the rug soaked in Randy's blood had been removed and was no longer an offense to eye or soul.

When I stepped into Randy's bedroom, I saw that Norella Mae had made the bed, as she no doubt had done in the guest bedroom also. And so in small details the effects of tragedy were beginning to fade from the scene.

I approached the kneehole writing desk in Randy's bedroom—rather larger than most such desks—with its four drawers on one side and four on the other.

In the top drawer on the right, I found a box of stationery bearing the letterhead: "Randol Hartwell, Broker in Works of Art and *Objets de Vertu.*"

Well, well! Why had I not known of this before?

Farther back in the drawer were several packets of letters held together by rubber bands, some of which had melted and stuck to the papers. From the dates on the postmarks and the contents of the few letters that I read, it appeared that Randy for a good many years had been carrying on negotiations of a covert nature for the owners of paintings, antiques, etc., who wished to sell such property with a minimum of public attention, either out of personal embarrassment or to conceal proceeds from the IRS. How Randy made contact with his clients, I did not discover. It was not necessary that I should know. But in the same drawer I found an address book containing the names of interior decorators in such cities as Cincinnati, Baltimore, and Philadelphia.

I am told that as the requirements of modern life have so greatly changed from those of our fathers' day, when sons and daughters leave ancestral households for more modest and convenient quarters, they are often at a loss to dispose of the family's acquired treasures without publicity: family portraits by known painters, too large to hang in a city apartment; monogrammed silver services far too extensive for the normal uses of modern hospitality; things of that sort.

Ergo Randy? Well, why not?

In the second drawer I found monogrammed stationery, personal correspondence, and bills, bills, bills, over which at another time I would have to pore intently. The third drawer contained what appeared to be the manuscript of an unfinished novel. Randy, the Renaissance man, obviously practiced all arts.

In the fourth drawer were folders of clippings from newspapers, etc. Also a reading glass and the remains of a desk set from which an ornamental lion had been broken. At the bottom of this detritus was an old-fashioned ledger book. It appeared to be a relic of Hartwell *père*'s early business activities.

In the top drawer on the other side was a telephone book, a few pencils, and a shoehorn. Why do we keep shoehorns? Everyone has at least one. We rarely use them, and when we happen to need one, we can't remember where it is.

The second drawer contained papers related to the genealogy of the Threadgils, Randy's mother's family.

In the third drawer I found five sample books of wallpaper of various dates and degrees of dinginess. They did not strike me as reflecting Randy's taste, but undoubtedly samplers are of value to the decorator. Perhaps they were part of a consignment of family treasures he had not been able to dispose of.

That left the fourth drawer. I pulled it out part way. At last it seemed that I had found what I was looking for: account books. These were the small personal account books that can be bought at any stationery shop or even at a drugstore. There were eight of them, covering the period from 1975 to the present.

I removed these account books and attempted to open the drawer further, but the confounded thing stuck. Leaning down to see what had caused the jam, I observed that in fact this drawer was considerably shorter than the others.

I muttered some expression of surprise and immediately removed the next drawer above in order to investigate.

Randy had rigged a "secret" compartment by the simple expedient of gluing a piece of wood across the lower drawer about two thirds of the distance from the front.

Then he had inserted screws in such a way that they stopped the removal of the drawer as though it had jammed in exactly the right place.

I could reach in, however, and extract the contents. Here was a stack of account books comparable to those I had found in the front of the drawer. They, too, began in 1975.

This was something to examine closely. A double set of books? If so, why? And why did Randy hide them like this? Did he think the IRS would conduct a search for them? If they or anyone else had done so, they would certainly have made the same discovery that I had made.

I knew that many an antique desk contained a secret compartment—mostly, I had always been told, to hide money from the servants. But Randy had not been hiding money. I decided this was a puzzle that I need not at the moment pursue.

I took both groups of account books as well as the letters I had found in the upper right-hand drawer home with me to study at my leisure. When I got around to examining them several days later, I found an interesting situation. The accounts from the books taken from the front of the drawer were kept neatly and in an apparently complete manner. They would seem to record Randy's income from all sources, each entry quite clear and beyond question. The other set of books, however, appeared to be in code. A comparison of the figures in the books from the rear of the drawer with those from the front did not immediately explain the mystery.

The administration of Randy's estate now appeared to me to be far more time-consuming than I could afford. There would be little gain in it for me—perhaps none except the possible discovery of a clue to the disposition of the portrait about which my wife was so interested.

Puzzles are the kind of thing my wife enjoys. And then

I thought of Mrs. Bushrow, in the nursing home recovering from a broken hip—Mrs. Bushrow, so good at mysteries! Here was more than a puzzle—here was a mystery. And Mrs. Bushrow was indeed our sleuth par excellence. Why not give all this material to her and let her keen old mind work out the solution?

Good idea!

My Bureau of Investigation

HARRIET GARDNER BUSHROW

There I was in the nursing home with a busted hip. Oh, I'm almost back to normal now. Those wonderful doctors got me nailed together again, and after a while I was able to whiz up and down the halls in my electrified wheelchair. After that, they began putting me on a walker. So I was making pretty good progress and I was looking forward to the time when I could drive my beautiful Buick that those sweet men in Rotary gave me. It's sitting there in my garage, and before too long I was determined to get home and get into that car and just drive and drive.

It would be dreadfully remiss of me if I didn't say right here that my friends were absolutely marvelous to me while I was in the nursing home. Margaret Chalmers, that sweet girl, took care of my houseplants for me. My little neighbor across the street who has always been so good to me saw that the boy came every week and cut my grass. And Lizzy Wheeler was just a saint—came by again and again, always with a slice of her delicious cakes or maybe with good cookies. I declare, I am ashamed I ever said anything bad about that girl.

And of course that darling Helen Delaporte, she was just an angel—and that nice husband of hers, too. You know we old ladies have our "gentlemen callers"—isn't that what Tennessee Williams called them?

I admit I had nothing to complain about there at the nursing home, but, oh how I did hate to be on the sidelines when there was all that excitement about Alberta's picture being stolen and Randy Hartwell being murdered! And yet, I followed it all, as you might say, from a distance.

So, when Helen brought me those account books of Randy's and those letters to see if I could figure out what it all meant, I said, "Dear child, just lay them up there on my bureau." Then I said, "Bureau! Of course. It's my Bureau of Investigation." And that's what we have been calling it ever since: Harriet's Bureau of Investigation—the HBI.

It didn't take long to puzzle out what Randy was up to, because, you see, there were dates in the account books and dates on the letters. They didn't match up exactly, but when I got the letters in chronological order, the dates on them were a few weeks or so earlier than the dates in the account books.

There would be a letter from a lady in Richmond wanting to sell a silver service that had been in the family for two hundred years—made in England, you know—and of course she didn't want people to know she had to sell it— so sad! And then in one of the account books there would be a date a month or so later and maybe an entry like $15,000.

And guess what? When I pointed this out to Henry Delaporte, he checked with the other account book, the one Randy kept to figure his income tax. And on the very same day that he wrote $15,000 in his secret book, that rascal would write something like $4,500 in the other book. No doubt that was what the poor little woman who was selling her family heirloom got, and no doubt she was gratified to get the money.

That Randy! But then, his mother brought him up all wrong. You can't go around telling a child he's a genius and whatever the darling wants to do is just fine. There is only one genius in a couple of million, and even a genius can do all kinds of mean, bad, evil things.

Well, I got that part of the mystery cleared up in a hurry—about the account books and the letters and all. And I figured that the initials in the secret account books were the initials of the firms that sold the silver or whatever.

Now you may say that the difference between the price at which those things were sold and the money Randy returned to the sellers was Randy's markup. Nonsense! Randy was just a conniving young rascal.

But to get on with my Bureau of Investigation. The Bible says those that have put their hand to the plow shouldn't turn back. If my mother preached that to me once, she did it a thousand times. And I guess the lesson took, for when I start something, I'm just like a bulldog—I won't let go of it till I have it finished and done with.

Now, an investigator is somebody who goes to the place where the information is and investigates. But a bureau is something else. That's where some people in an office receive reports and go over them and compare them and get everything concentrated and coordinated and all worked out. Right?

Well, in this Historical Society mystery, we had what you might call operatives in the field. There was Helen, of course, and Henry Delaporte—and that nice Mr. Robert Kelsey that used to wait on me at the post office. And I'm not forgetting the police on the Tennessee side.

Of course the police couldn't share their information with just anybody, but they had made statements to the *Banner-Democrat*. And so I count them as my operatives because I had what they had said in those articles.

Now Mercy knows I had lots of time to run my "bureau" and sort out every little piece of information that came to me. So, little by little I began to get things straight in my head.

Well, to get the facts in order, I'll put it like this:

The Historical Society goes to get the picture of that French king that Alberta Chamberlain left to them in her will, and it turns out not to be the real thing.

Helen Delaporte gives the story to those people at the *Banner-Democrat*, and they put it in the paper that the real picture was worth a million dollars.

The next thing we know, there's another story in the *Banner-Democrat* that Randy Hartwell has been found nude and stabbed to death with an antique dagger. The story says there are indications that someone had slept in the guest room that night.

Then Mr. Kelsey discovers an intruder in Randy's house and finds a piece of the giltwork broken from the frame of Alberta's picture, and next morning he learns that the intruder was Randy's great-nephew, that nineteen-year-old Spud Shankley.

Then he learns that Spud helped Randy take Alberta's picture out of the house while she was in the hospital and returned it the same night. Then, a few weeks later, the two of them went to Alberta's house and took the picture to Randy's house again. Randy carried it into the house, leaving young Spud waiting somewhere while Randy and the picture disappeared for a while. Half an hour later Randy came back with the forged copy of the painting, which he had put into the frame that was originally on the picture when it was at Alberta's house.

So it seems that Randy intended to sell the painting— oh, at some far-off place where he could be sure that folks like us would never know about it—and the poor Historical Society would just have the frame and a worthless picture.

Now, I thought about that quite a while—that is, "my bureau evaluated the evidence"—and two things came to mind. One is that Randy had this theft in view for a good many years.

You see, it would probably have been a long time ago that he got hold of Alberta's key—most likely at the time he was playing for the charity teas she used to put on. He undoubtedly had the whole thing planned back then. But while Alberta was in the house, he couldn't do a thing about it. I don't know what he would have done if she had died at home. But, you see, they took her to the hospital, and that gave him his chance.

I imagine Randy had kept up with Alberta pretty closely—taking little things to her, flowers and so on—so that he would know when he would have a chance to pull off his shenanigans.

Now the question is: How did he get a painting to substitute for the original? I figured he must have taken a photograph of the painting the first time he had that picture at his home, and then right there in his own house he had someone make the copy.

That was the first conclusion of my Bureau of Investigation. And I told Mr. Delaporte, "Look in Randy's house for a photograph or slide of that painting," because, after all, he had his hands on the real painting and was alone with it for something less than an hour before he substituted the copy for the original.

And goodness knows it would take something like a month to paint a copy that would fool anybody—or at least I would think it would.

Now, I know that there are artists that go to museums

and copy paintings fair and square, and it's like a profession to them. When we lived in Washington, I used to know a lady who did that. But if we had anybody like her in Borderville, I never heard of it.

So I asked myself whether Randy could have made a photograph and sent it away to be copied by an artist.

You've probably seen ads of people who do mail-order copy work. You know: "Send us a snapshot of your loved one or pet and we will make you a beautiful life-size oil painting of same—satisfaction guaranteed."

I saw a painting from one of those places once, and the results wouldn't have satisfied *me*. But whoever did the copying for Randy must have been good at it—a real professional.

We are talking about a great big painting, and how would the person who did the copying get it back to Randy just in the nick of time before Alberta died? And then, too, suppose the copy was made somewhere out of town and delivered to Randy by private van. In that case, as soon as Randy had made the substitution of the copy for the real portrait, he could have sent the real portrait away in the same van, and that would be why nobody could find it. In that case, though, the theft of the painting would have nothing to do with Randy's death.

After all, I just had to think that there was a painter in Borderville who had made the copy. But who could it be? Could Randy do it himself? I asked Helen about that, and she said the only paintings of his she had seen were that nonobjective stuff. I can tell you that didn't sound like what the lady in Washington did—the lady that made the copies at the museum there.

There had to be somebody in Borderville who could fill the order for Randy: take a photograph and make a bang-up good copy of it. But if there was, he surely had been keeping his light under a bushel. Otherwise everybody in town would know about it.

Then I had to ask myself how important was it to know who painted the fake, or how he did it, or where he lived? Wasn't the main thing for us to find the real painting? The other question about who killed Randy Hartwell might or might not relate to our search for the stolen picture. But somehow I just felt it in my bones that the two things went together.

Of course the story in the paper made it look like the police thought Randy was killed in some kind of sex episode. That was mostly because Randy's body was nude and the murder weapon seemed to be something that belonged to Randy and just happened to be at hand when the murderer had a fit of anger, picked it up, and stuck it into Randy's back.

I didn't think sex had anything to do with it. Helen reported that Randy's bed had been slept in by just one person. And just one person slept in the guest room. And who was to say that Randy didn't have the habit of sleeping nude? I understand many people do that.

Still, the list of guests Randy had at his party—and no doubt the police in their investigation had learned a great deal more about the party than we were likely to learn—now that was a strange list of guests. And the information about them that Bob Kelsey got from that boy Spud would support what the police were thinking.

I know sex causes lots of trouble—lots of crimes and so on. But money causes just as many. And as soon as the *Banner-Democrat* printed that story to the effect that the picture was worth a million dollars, anybody who knew that Randy had the real picture automatically became a suspect. That would mean the person who copied the picture, or somebody who by hook or by crook knew that Randy had the thing—perhaps any of those people who were at the party. Now, there was one person at the party who knew about the picture. That was Spud. But he was with his girl while Randy was being murdered. And the one who made the copy knew about the picture, and maybe somebody else knew, too.

It boils down to this: Of the persons who may have wanted to get that portrait away from Randy to sell it and could have done so, the only one we could be sure of was the artist who made the copy.

I explained all of this—that is, my Bureau of Investigation put out an "all-points bulletin" about it—and urged Mr. Delaporte to make a thorough search of the house for a photographic negative or a slide. I didn't know where that would take us. But at least it would be a start.

Mission Accomplished

HENRY DELAPORTE

The very next day after I received Mrs. Bushrow's suggestion, I visited Randy's basement photographic studio to
trace his activities there.

I know nothing of cameras, and even if I had been moderately knowledgeable, I should have been out of my depth.
Apparently Randy's determination to practice all the arts
had found its most elaborate outlet in photography.

I located five cameras of the kind we might expect to see
hanging from the necks of paparazzi. All looked expensive,
and each, I am sure, had been bought for some arcane and
highly specialized purpose.

There was also a large tripod-mounted camera of the sort
that is used in professional photographic studios. In addition, I found lighting equipment that would be hard for me
to describe, and equipment of the sort that we often see in
department stores when Olin Mills makes the rounds—
those roller gadgets from which the photographer can pull
various sheets to provide backgrounds for his pictures.

In the same area of the basement, I found a metal cabinet, the top drawer of which contained photographic prints,
mostly eight-by-ten. There were European scenes, local
shots of our incomparable scenery, shots of stray cats, nest-

ing birds, and the like. And then there were portraits—quite a number, some of which I recognized immediately as likenesses of local persons. I laid these aside on the basis that they might furnish us with a longer roster of possible suspects.

Finally I came to a very interesting collection: Randy's studies of the nude.

Randy had obviously been impressed by the late Robert Mapplethorpe. Of the various models, I immediately concluded from the general bulge of muscle that one was our bodybuilder, Tony Braun.

The pictures were well lighted, and obviously the camera had captured every detail in absolute clarity. Perhaps that was the flaw. The effect was nothing to compare with the achievement of the great photographers. Moreover, the poses, even to my untrained eye, simply didn't have it.

Staid, almost stolid, and certainly chaste—at least the ones that first came to light—these pictures resembled only too closely photographs of ancient statuary. The only thing embarrassing about them was Tony Braun's pretending to be the Discus-Thrower.

Given the local assumption regarding Randy's sexual orientation, what followed was a surprise: studies of the female nude—various models in various poses.

There were in the neighborhood of forty prints. But they seemed almost to have been taken by a different photographer. Although not in the style of *Playboy* or *Penthouse,* all of the female nudes were faintly pornographic.

One in particular proved to be of special interest. Curled up on a sofa, over which something that appeared to be a Spanish shawl had been thrown, was a somewhat plump woman—not at all young in appearance—naked except for patent leather high-heeled shoes. The rouge on her parted lips was smeared and the mascara about her eyes was exaggerated. There was nothing conventionally attractive about the body or the face. And yet the shiny black shoes, the dead white flesh, the smear of red on the lips, and the huge eyes staring from their artificially black lashes produced a shocking effect.

I shuffled back to the male nudes. A few of the photos involved two nude male figures. To what extent were they erotic? As I looked at them, I somehow got the feeling that the models were either embarrassed or so unused to posing for the camera that Randy's intentions could not possibly have been achieved. One of the prints, I recall, appeared to show two men wrestling—perhaps again a pose suggested by some antique or Renaissance original. Another showed two naked men standing side by side, arms across shoulders—a pose reminding me of a snapshot of myself and my younger brother, fully clothed, taken on my sixth birthday. Aside from the nudity, Randy's choice of pose was hardly different from the one Ed and I had been persuaded to assume so many years ago.

You may think me something of a Peeping Tom for examining these prints in such detail. It would be hard to claim that the greater part of them impinged on our pursuit of the stolen canvas. There was the possibility that they were related in some way to the murder—particularly as they seemed to shed light of some sort on the police assumption that Randy's death had a homosexual angle. However that might be, I challenge anyone coming upon such a collection not to look.

I did indeed look at them, rather closely. And to my surprise—no, shock!—I suddenly recognized the loan officer at my bank . . . embracing another nude male! Whereas I had not been embarrassed before, now I felt blood pulsing under the band of my collar. Poor Bill Holder! That slack body of his! I felt that even I, clothed only as God made me, would have looked better—more fit—more virilely handsome.

Then I looked back at the woman curled up on the Spanish shawl—and wasn't that the shawl that was under the vase on the Bösendorfer upstairs? Her body varied quite as far from the ideal as did Bill's. And yet I recognized her as sexy. Obviously attraction, like beauty, is in the eye of the beholder.

But the face—wiped clean of the rouge and mascara, without that leer—would I have recognized it then? Or had I looked at it so long that it seemed familiar?

I shuffled back to the portrait prints, and there indeed was the same face—a woman fashionably dressed, wearing a long string of pearls knotted to shorten the scope. The intention here seemed to be an imitation of Cecil Beaton, and Randy had failed even as he had failed to capture the spirit of Mapplethorpe.

I turned the picture over hesitantly. There, penciled on the back of it, I read: "Erindell, Oct. 10, '82."

Erindell Schovall, our East Tennessee poet! I looked again at the nude pose. Randy's intention there seemed all too clear. But it was also preposterous.

Was there something in this that I was missing? I seemed to remember that Erindell Schovall was a Deeds from Deedsville, whatever degree of family connection that might suggest. And somewhere in the back of my mind lurked something picked up while tracing a title several years ago. I had the impression of wealth in the Deeds family.

Had that wealth ever been available to Randy through Erindell Schovall? Would he have married her for it?

Then of course he might have gotten some of her money without having to marry the woman. There must have been some fantasy love life, perhaps something of a Bohemian fling with Randy, or there would be no explanation for the nude photo. No matter how the woman might have viewed the affair, she would not want that photograph made public.

No more would Holder desire to have his naked body shown to the depositors of the Volunteer Bank and Trust Co.

Perhaps here was a motive for murder.

Let us suppose that there were other, more compromising pictures of Holder. Randy, being in dire straits and having planned his escape through the sale of a genuine portrait by Charles Willson Peale—and finding his plan compromised or at least postponed through my wife's discovery of the scam—could have used a compromising photo of the loan officer to postpone a calamity that would have robbed him of his Alfa Romeo, his Bösendorfer, and even his extravagant house.

Or in the case of Erindell Schovall, might he not have recourse to an embarrassing and indeed incriminating photo hidden away in a metal cabinet in his basement? Had he put it to use, one wonders how many ladies' clubs would fête the sweet singer of East Tennessee and listen with rapture to her melodious lines. Would she be disgraced? Or worse, would she be rendered merely silly? I suspect the latter would disturb the lady more.

But back to those two nude brethren, looking so foolish in their naked state. I had recognized the one as the loan officer who could be very helpful to Randy if properly persuaded. Was the other Torrence?

With the exception of the naked Erindell curled up on that Spanish shawl, none of these photos would be called hard core. But perhaps there had been others, shots that Randy had kept in a safer place—or perhaps just the negatives.

It does very well to say that there is an open climate for

accepting homosexuality. It does equally well to point to open discussion and even portrayal of homosexuality on the television screen or in the movies. And it does very well to point to nationally prominent figures who are out of the closet. But to be outed unwillingly must be extremely unpleasant, and nowhere could it be less pleasant than in Borderville, Virginia-Tennessee.

What I had found in Randy's photographic files so far seemed to strengthen the police position that Randy's murder most likely resulted from something connected with his sexual proclivities. So far, my discovery led away from the theft of the portrait, and obfuscated rather than clarified our view of the case as opposed to that of the police. But I had not yet examined the next-lower drawer.

It creaked open to reveal several square boxes containing carousels of photographic slides. I wondered what further interest they might provide.

Fortunately, the gear I needed to view these slides remained where Randy apparently had left it. The projector on its stand was plugged in. I had merely to put the carousel in place, pull down a screen conveniently hanging from the ceiling, and I was in business. I flipped the switch on the projector and doused the lights. There, with the very first slide, was the likeness of Louis-Philippe thrown in clear detail on the screen.

Mrs. Bushrow had been absolutely correct. This was how the picture had been copied.

And yet we were no further than we had been before. We had known from Spud's statement that Randy was the culprit as regards the theft of the portrait.

But perhaps there was something new here. Knowing the method by which the painting had been copied, could we perhaps find out who had done the copying?

I knew nothing of painting, but it struck me that here was

a short-cut method that would make the task much quicker, and easier. I recalled a craze some years ago for painting-by-the-numbers. It struck me that here was something of the same sort. Perhaps by use of the slide, the picture could be copied effectively by a lesser talent than would otherwise be required.

In short, someone with a keen eye for color and skill in its application, and yet with no very great capacity for drawing, might have done the work.

I thought of the nonobjective paintings by Randy that I had seen upstairs. I recalled also that Helen had pointed out to me that the rich colors had been coordinated with the various shades in the Oriental carpets lying nearest each of the canvases.

I wondered if, after all, Randy himself had created the copy?

I proceeded to examine the other slides on the carousel.

These slides were individually different, but clearly and curiously related. I would look at a slide and see a flower arrangement. The next slide would show a canvas supported by a table and propped against the wall—the very table, in fact, that stood in the corner of the room in which I stood. The flowers painted on the canvas resembled those in the preceding slide, but with a pronounced difference. They stood out in clear light against a very dark background. The colors were intensified, if anything. In short, these were the same flowers in a slightly different arrangement, given a completely different aspect. This was almost, but not quite, "painting-by-the-numbers."

There were a good many of these slides—different arrangements with different flowers—always a photograph of the actual flowers accompanied by another photograph recording the painting made from the same arrangement.

Other objects appeared in the paintings that had not been in the arrangements when the actual flowers had been photographed. Among these objects, I realized with a shock, was an antique dagger, which must have been the one with which Randy was killed.

I found these slides so curious that I took them home with me and showed them to Helen.

She put them into our projector, drew the curtains shut, and threw the images on the wall.

"Seventeenth-century Flemish," she pronounced.

I smiled. "Twentieth-century Borderville," I said. I rarely had an opportunity to correct my wife.

Helen viewed each of the slides with great attention and interest.

"Amazing," she said, when she had completed her examination. "I dare say the idea was Randy's, but I can't believe the execution was his."

I agreed, though I couldn't put my reasons for doing so into words. "Please explain," I demanded.

"Because," Helen replied, "he hasn't the discipline. I have heard him play the piano, please remember, and there was no discipline there. I can't believe there would be any in his painting."

Elated with our discovery, we "celebrated" by having dinner at Ted's, the excellent Greek restaurant we are fortunate enough to have here in Borderville. And as usual, my cup was filled too frequently with Ted's strong black coffee.

Which, of course, has nothing to do with the story except that the coffee kept me awake until the not-so-wee hours of the following morning.

I do not regret sleepless nights. In the complicated world of the present, it is a privilege to be alone and to enjoy one's own thoughts. Hence my easy tolerance of sleepless nights, for one is never more completely alone than when he finds himself awake in the dark in a comfortable bed within the walls of his own room.

The phone will not ring, or at least it is unlikely to do so. A client will not come in. For a wonderful, relaxed while, I can't take out the garbage, I can't reconcile my checkbook or attend to any petty occupations of the day. I am left to the companionship of my own thoughts.

And I almost always enjoy the companionship of my own thoughts.

On this occasion, my thoughts reviewed the adventure of the preceding afternoon. I found myself again in Randy's basement. With curious clarity, details came back to me. There were the file cabinets in which I had found those very interesting photographs. I could even see the light glinting from their gray metallic sides—and next to them the projector on its stand aimed at the opposite wall. I had to think that it had not been moved since—well, since Randy had thrown the image of Peale's painting on the new canvas for tracing.

But wait! I had pulled down a screen hanging from the ceiling. That screen had nothing to do with the process of tracing the picture. The canvas must have been set on an easel—and the easel? Yes, there had been an easel in that basement—in the corner to the left of the projector.

Why had I been so stupid? I had handled the carousel in which I had found the slides—I had even brought it home. The fingerprints on it would be mine.

And in placing the carousel on Randy's projector, I had probably obliterated the earlier prints that may have been left there.

But the easel—I had not touched it.

Surely the artist who copied the portrait of Louis-

Philippe must have left fingerprints there. Surely the police should examine that easel.

Next morning, first thing after I arrived at the office, I called Chief Runnels and suggested that Don Cochran, the department detective, should look for fingerprints on the easel in Randy's basement. Runnels was agreeable, and we made arrangements for me to meet Cochran at the Hartwell place that afternoon.

Between us, we made a complete inspection of the basement. The easel I had supposed might have been used in producing the fraudulent painting, upon scrutiny, was obviously too small to accommodate a six-foot canvas.

Cochran, however, aware now of the method by which the projector had been used, surmised that some kind of temporary scaffolding had been used to hold the canvas— perhaps secured to the rings that held Randy's roll-up screens to the ceiling, the screens he used in his photography.

We searched the place thoroughly for such a scaffolding and found it at length—four two-by-fours lying at the side of the house which, up to that point, I had not inspected, the side farthest from the street.

Nailholes indicated the manner in which these timbers had been assembled, and the size and arrangement confirmed the use to which they had been put. There were even smudges of paint on the wood.

Sadly, Officer Cochran informed me that the rain that had fallen the previous week would certainly have destroyed all fingerprints on the lumber. Nevertheless, he dusted everything that in any way might provide interesting prints.

What a pity that his report several days later was unable to find prints that were not Randy's, Cochran's, or mine.

Data on the Borderville Art Colony

HARRIET GARDNER BUSHROW

That sweet Helen brought her projector and some of those slides Henry found and showed them to me in the nursing home. I must say, I found them very interesting. Seventeenth century, she said those flower pictures looked like! Now you know that Randy didn't paint those himself, and he didn't have them painted to give away to his friends. No, indeed. He had an art racket going on, and it had been going on for some time. Stealing the portrait of King Louis was just the latest wrinkle in a scheme he had been working for years.

I was interested in what Helen had to say about Erindell Schovall, too, and that dear little fellow down at the bank and his pal. But pshaw! I don't believe for a minute they— or anyone like them—either killed Randy or got off with Alberta's picture.

So the next thing for me to do was to turn my attention to the artists who live somewhere close around here.

By chance—and I find that is the way things usually happen—Luella Mellursh is right here in this nursing home. She is a bright little thing, no bigger than a minute—just skin and bones, but very careful about the way she dresses: always has a little blue chiffon scarf tied around her neck with a bow under one ear. Maybe that will tell you what color her eyes are: blue!

Anyhow, the point is that Luella taught art in the public schools here for forty-five years. Now, I think anybody who has done all that deserves to have her statue in the park.

I was beginning to use a walker to get around, and that made it possible for me to walk right in and sit down beside her in the nice, big room they have here with lots of windows and sunlight.

I started our conversation by saying, "I know you must miss your art terribly." She has arthritis, you know.

"Yes," she said, "but sometimes we have to look back and be glad that once upon a time we could do those things that gave us so much pleasure, even though we can't do them anymore."

Now wasn't that a beautiful thing to say!

"I imagine you painted oh so many pictures," I said.

"Hundreds of them—oils, watercolor, pastel. . . ."

"Where are they now?"

"Oh," she said, "I gave them away. So many of the ones I gave them to are gone now. But perhaps someone has kept them."

That is something old folks have to think about. Where does the work of our lives go? I really didn't know what to say next. But after a little pause, she went on.

"It was the painting itself and being out of doors—I did landscapes mostly—that's what I really enjoyed. All those scenes I painted are fixed in my mind, you know."

I knew exactly what she meant. We need to live so that when we are crippled up and can't do things anymore, our memories will be good company. And I lived that way—mostly—though I have my regrets, too. But we won't go into that.

"I know it's wonderful," I said, "to think of the hundreds of children that have gone through your classes. To think how you have brought out the talent in this one and that one!"

"There is nothing as exciting as a talented student."

Luella made me feel ashamed. Here I was asking her this and that and the other thing to get her to talk about Randy Hartwell. You would think I wasn't at all interested in Luella—which I suppose I really wasn't. It is not the nicest thing in the world to go around fishing for information that is none of my business. But I went right on doing it.

"Talent is so rare," I said. "Did you ever have Randy Hartwell in your class?"

"Indeed I did," she replied.

I couldn't tell from the tone of her voice just how I ought to take that.

"And he was very talented, I'm sure," I suggested.

"I think," she said—and then hesitated. "Perhaps *ambitious* would be a better word."

There! I had my answer. But I wanted more.

"Oh, surely ambitious! But he had talent in so many ways—his music and so on. And you don't think he had much talent in art?"

"It was rather pathetic," Luella began. "I have never seen another child who wanted to be praised so constantly. He seemed to think he had a right to it."

I had to agree with that, but I didn't comment.

"You know," she continued, "the other children had their simple little watercolor boxes—black and white, yellow, green, blue, purple, red, and orange. But Randy had a set of watercolors that a professional would have found very desirable.

"And he would paint things at home and bring them to me.

"Of course, any teacher likes to see interest in a student, and the work wasn't bad, but I did not think he did it out of love of art. He wanted me to approve of *him*. And I always said something nice about everything he did. It would have been cruel not to.

"He was always bringing me flowers and so on. And he was such a neat child, and so polite.

"But the most talented child I ever had in class was Randy's little friend, Charlie Gunn. You know, his mother had the florist's shop."

Luella knew Mrs. Gunn and about how she is in very bad health and Charlie is not having an easy time of it. We talked about that for a while. But I soon turned the conversation back to Charlie's talent. That was the thing I was interested in—this boyhood friend of Randy, and still his friend, and at Randy's house the evening before Randy was killed. And now I was finding out that Charlie was the best art student Luella ever taught.

She called him her star pupil, very quick to learn, so good with watercolors and good at drawing, too. He went on with his painting although he never had any formal training other than what Luella taught him. She said he still paints—in watercolors—flowers. "After all," she observed, "he is in the floral business."

Watercolors—I wasn't interested in watercolors! "Does he ever paint in oils?" I asked.

"Oh, he may have tried it once or twice, but watercolor is definitely his true love. He exhibits every year—wins ribbons too. Almost always paints flowers, you see."

Yes, I did see. Painting flowers was very interesting. But from what Luella was saying, although Charlie Gunn might have been able to paint flowers in watercolors, I didn't think the flower pictures in those slides Helen had told me about were watercolor. And that six-foot-tall painting of King Louis certainly was no water-color.

Well, we talked on. I managed to insert into the conversation all the other people who were at Randy's party the night he was murdered. Luella didn't react to any of them, though she knew Maybelle Sprote, the one that makes the pottery things. And when I dropped the name of Erindell Schovall into the discussion, Luella exclaimed, "Oh, that's the woman from Deedsville who writes the poetry," and she didn't sound like she cared very much for the poetry.

Then I launched into other waters—still fishing, you see. I said, "I think I have heard of some kind of art club or organization for artists here. Are you a member?" Of course I knew it was the Borderville Art League, but I wanted Luella to tell me about it.

And she did. Before the conversation was over, I had the names of three people she considered excellent in oil painting. These were Frederick Woodcott, Princess Poulter, and Judith Wexler.

I am well aware that just because Luella doesn't know about it, that is no reason to suppose that Charlie Gunn isn't as good at oils as he is at watercolors. And just because Maybelle Sprote makes jugs and such things, there is no reason to think she can't paint. So there may be other people in town who could furnish Randy with a satisfactory copy of Alberta's picture.

All the same, if I had been on my two feet the way I ought to be, I would have figured out a way to talk to Gunn and Sprote as well as Woodcott, Poulter, and Wexler.

But since I was just beginning to use the walker, and since I was merely running a Bureau of Investigation, I gave the names to Helen Delaporte and commissioned her to find out what she could about each of these people.

Tony Braun

HENRY DELAPORTE

Randy's financial affairs were so utterly tangled and his records so incomplete and/or deceptive that I was a long time working at them. Meanwhile, to be sure, I had other and more pressing matters to attend to at the office. It seemed therefore a good idea to keep the Hartwell papers at Randy's house, where I could work on them at the desk in Randy's bedroom. Then, when I left off for a day or two, they would be undisturbed and I could find them again just where I had put them.

The house was only ten minutes from my office. Whenever I had an hour or so, I could buzz over and do whatever work I had time for. Thus I was in and out of the place at various times, usually in the late afternoon.

One day, however, an appointment was canceled for a one o'clock meeting with a client; thus I arrived at Randy's house considerably earlier than I had done before.

It was a sunny, warm day. I parked, of course, in the carport and entered through the kitchen. Finding the house intolerably stuffy, I went to open a number of doors and windows. When I started to open the French doors in the living room, I was in for a surprise.

Lying naked poolside was a two-hundred-twenty-pound

mass composed of muscle, bone, and deeply tanned skin. It was obviously Tony Braun.

Reconnoitering briefly before opening the doors, I saw a ten-speed bicycle leaning against the wall surrounding the pool area; from its frame hung a not entirely white T-shirt, a pair of faded blue athletic shorts, and a jockstrap. Nearby on the flagstones were an iridescent biker's helmet and a pair of running shoes into which white socks had been tucked.

How had this hulk gotten into the enclosure? Obviously through the door in the wall, which I had not noticed before. And what should I do about it?

Tony looked as if he was very much at home—comfortable and relaxed, lying there on his back with dark glasses protecting his eyes. He was doing no harm—certainly no more harm than a stray dog that might come on the premises and do exactly what Tony was doing. Why, then, should I object?

I opened the door and stepped outside.

"Hello, there."

Tony reared slightly on one elbow and craned his neck in my direction.

"You must be Tony Braun."

"Yeah, that's me."

"How did you get in here?"

"Well, I have a key."

At that I came closer and sat on one of the deck chairs.

"I'm Henry Delaporte."

"Yeah."

"Well, I'm also executor of the estate of the late Randol Hartwell."

Tony didn't say anything.

"Does your key open the house doors as well as the gate here?"

"Yeah—sure."

"I understand that Mr. Hartwell allowed you to use this area for tanning purposes." That was something I had learned from Spud Shankley.

"That's right."

"I suppose we could let you continue to use this area, but I'm a little nervous that there are so many keys around. Spud has one, I have one, and now I find that you have one. You are brown as a tea stain already. Why do you have to be so tan?"

He explained that competing bodybuilders have no chance in competitions unless they have a deep, all-over tan. Whether that is true or not is immaterial. What is material is that he was seeking advancement in a field that I do not at all understand. His modest little gym with its small clientele of would-be Sandows hardly supported him at all. Witness the bicycle, his only means of transportation, which, though it was health-promoting and athletic, did not, I should imagine, satisfy his soul the way a neat sports car would have done.

As Tony was explaining his circumstances to me, it occurred to him to roll over and lie on his belly.

"How about slapping some oil on my back?" he said.

I am sixty-five years old. I am Senior Warden of Saint Luke's Episcopal Church. I had never before laid eyes on this young man, who was several years younger than my youngest child. And here he was asking me to smear tanning oil on his naked back.

I squatted beside the prone figure. The bottle of tanning oil—the type that ensures the deepest tan—appeared greasy. But I took it up anyhow and prepared to slather it on those broad shoulders.

"You know, you have your nerve," I observed.

I felt the muscular reaction as he started to lift his head to answer me.

"Never mind," I said. "I'm oiling you anyhow. How did you get to know Randy?"

It had been the preceding summer, soon after Tony opened his gym, he told me. He was on his bicycle coasting down the hill on Johnston Street over on the Virginia side, when an Alfa Romeo passed him. It was the first time he had seen the Alfa Romeo, and he was impressed.

At the bottom of the hill the Alfa Romeo stopped for a traffic light, and the driver hailed Tony when he came abreast.

"Do you ever model?" Randy had asked through his open window.

Tony had been somewhat confused. He had never modeled—he supposed it would be ads for clothing or something similar—and he would be delighted to get into work of that sort.

When the light changed, both men drew over to the curb in the next block and negotiated an agreement.

What Randy wanted, as I already knew, was someone to pose for his camera. After some discussion, it was agreed that Randy would pay minimum wage and Tony could have free use of the prints for any publicity he might want.

That was only the beginning. I gathered that the magnificent symmetry of Tony's body alone did not make him by nature the ideal model. But Randy had ideas about posing that greatly impressed Tony, and it was not long before Randy was giving the bodybuilder rudimentary lessons in ballet.

"And that improved your posing?" I asked.

"Oh, yes. Let me show you."

With that he got up and went through a series of postures—obviously a routine—which not only showed his muscles to advantage but suggested real athletic grace. Tony became not just a congeries of bumps and lumps, as bodybuilders seem often to be; he had, instead, an agility and power like that of the big cats I used to admire so much at the *Clyde Beatty Show*.

I questioned Tony as to whether anyone else had a key to the house. He said he didn't know. We finally concluded that he could retain the key and use the poolside as he pleased, with the understanding that he was strictly responsible and that nobody else was to use it. There was, after all, some property there by the pool—a table with an umbrella sprouting from its center and several chairs. Even though Tony promised to keep the gate locked, I was a little nervous about the key.

Somewhat later, as the reader will learn, I was amazed at the number of keys Randy had passed out. In fact, I was to think almost that I was at a revival of that old play *Seven Keys to Baldpate*. But all turned out well in the end, and the friendly relations I established with Tony Braun by oiling his naked back, allowing him free use of the pool area, and trusting him with a key paid off in several ways, one of which I shall now explain.

As I have implied, there was a normal press of business at the office and no hurry about the Hartwell estate. Consequently, there were more days than not when I altogether ignored my duties at Randy's house.

Much has been said about "the law's delays," but let me assure the reader that there is reason for them.

And so I did not see Tony more than one or two more times until well into June. Whenever I saw him, he was baking himself in the sun. He left no litter and did no harm. And on the whole it was probably better having him on the place now and then, checking, as it were. I was confident of course that he would report to me anything that was amiss.

The third week in June was hotter than blazes. It was so

hot that I had to force myself to leave my air-conditioned office and go out to Randy's place.

When I got there, I found Tony, naked as the day he was born, splashing about in the pool.

I opened the French doors and said, "That looks so good I'd like to do it myself."

"Why don't you?" he replied.

Why not indeed? I remembered the pleasures of the swimming hole near my grandfather's farm in Louisiana, where I spent my summers as a boy. Swimming completely naked is so different from swimming in a suit! And what could be more private than Randy's pool?

The water was invitingly clear, and the bottom of the pool was painted blue.

I took off my tie, then my shirt, then everything else. The slight breeze felt cool and wonderful. Also cool and wonderful was the feel of the water on my bare flesh when I dived in with a most gratifying splash.

The pool was too small for swimming, but we bounced around in it as people do in backyard pools. After a while Tony got out and laid himself down on the beach towel that he had brought with him.

I too left the pool, but I had no towel.

"Here, take mine," Tony offered.

I protested that I could do no such thing. And yet, dripping as I was, I could neither put on my clothes nor go into the house for a towel. In the end I lay down on the flagstones.

At first they were very hot, but they were quite smooth, and as the sun relaxed my body, a pleasant feeling stole over me.

"Would you like some of my suntan oil?" Tony offered.

"I don't need anything to make me tan," I replied. "I need something to keep me from burning."

"Here," he said. "Just put it all over you."

As I anointed myself, he returned to his beach towel on the other side of the pool.

"Is your gym air-conditioned?" I asked as I lay back down.

"Hell no!" he assured me. "It is hotter'n a firecracker." Lying there, with the pool between us of course, we were very companionable. He told me about his high school and how he was a line blocker on the varsity. He had been one year at college on an athletic scholarship, but the required courses had been too much for him. Perhaps if he had tried at some other college where he would not have had to take math and all those things. . . . His voice trailed off.

His monologue resumed and bubbled on rather pleasantly. It required no concentration on my part to listen.

Then suddenly:

"You know, Randy wasn't rich like most people thought."

Had even Tony, who found math difficult along with some other things, actually observed this fact? I was sure that Randy would have hidden his difficulties with a finesse very difficult for someone like Tony to penetrate.

"Why do you say that?" I prompted.

"It was four days—no, three days—before, you know, when—when Randy got killed."

"Go on."

"I was out here. It was a great day for the rays, and it was warm. That was why the doors were open.

"I don't think he knew I was here, because I didn't come in through the house or anything.

"Anyhow, I was out here, and he was in there, and it was real quiet. He was talkin' on the phone. It seemed like somebody wanted some money—but they couldn't get together on it."

My interest increased remarkably. In fact, I sat up. "Tony!" I said. "Do you think you can remember exactly what was said?" It was too much to expect. It was now over a month since the event. But even a snatch of Randy's end of the conversation might help.

"Well, I think . . ." Tony began, "I think the first thing I heard was, 'We had an agreement.' Yes, that was it. 'We had an agreement, and that's all you are going to get.' "

There was a lapse. "And then . . . ?" I prompted.

"Well, then the other person had quite a lot to say. And Randy came back: 'Ten thousand dollars and not a cent more.' "

I was amazed at the apparent detail with which Tony was recounting the conversation. Certainly the accuracy was suspect. But perhaps a mind uncluttered with the mental baggage most of us carry could retain many of the phrases of a conversation that had been surprising at the time and might well have been further entrenched by the sensations of Randy's murder soon after.

My attention was riveted, as you may imagine, to every word Tony was ostensibly recalling. Randy had had an altercation only shortly before his death.

"And then," Tony continued, "Randy said, 'No! You agreed on ten thousand. And I don't even have that much.' And next it was: 'Well, it's not going to auction. It's your fault, you know. You'll get your ten thousand, but you'll have to wait.' "

"Was there any more?"

"Oh, yes," Tony said, "but a big truck went by and I couldn't hear all of it. But when I could hear again, he was saying, 'Fifty-fifty? Don't be a fool! It may be ten years before it will be safe to move it, and I don't know what I will do until then.'

"Then there was something I didn't catch. After that he

said real loud, 'Don't you understand! I have debt up to my tits.' Then it was: 'Just take it easy. I think I know where I can get a little, and if she comes through, maybe I can give you something on account.' Then the person on the other end must have said something that really rang Randy's number, because he said, 'Damn you! If you ever get anything, it will be ten thousand and not another cent.' And he slammed down the phone."

This conversation could only have taken place between Randy and his accomplice in the theft of Mrs. Chamberlain's painting. We had already determined that Randy made a habit of deceiving other parties in almost every deal we had been able to trace. Obviously, he had tried it again. He had contracted with the copyist for ten thousand dollars. The copyist, no doubt, was unaware of the potential value of the Peale canvas. The *Banner-Democrat* story had been an epiphany— a revelation that cut like a knife between Randy and his accomplice.

I had formed an idea of the extent of Randy's indebtedness. The house was mortgaged. He had taken a loan on the Bösendorfer. The Alfa Romeo had been bought secondhand, and it too was unpaid for.

Randy had set himself up as a genius; he was, I had concluded, a genius in the skill with which he shuffled his finances. It appeared that at last his sins might have found him out.

Deep as he was in debt, what a sigh of relief he must have breathed when he learned of Mrs. Chamberlain's fatal sickness. But then to have the theft revealed through the accident of my wife's friendship with Genevieve and Sterling Brenthauser—how deeply must Randy have felt that blow! There was no way by which he could sell the Peale canvas at anything like its real value. The million-dollar estimate which Brenthauser had put upon the painting might or might not be accurate. However, no matter what the portrait's real value might be, after it had passed through the hands of fences and who knows how many other connivers, just consider how much the payment Randy would receive would have shrunk!

I don't know how Randy expected to hide the eventual transaction from the IRS, but that could only be an academic question, so we can forget about it.

However I looked at it, Randy had been a desperate man. The game was about to be up. He was going to lose everything. It was merely ironic that he lost his life before he lost the house, the Alfa Romeo, and the Bösendorfer.

And then in his last hours to be dunned by an accomplice—poetic justice!

" 'If *she* comes through?' " I repeated a snatch of the conversation. "You are sure that is what he said? 'She'?"

"That's what he said."

"Do you have any idea who 'she' could be?"

"Well, I *did* wonder. There's this real old woman that was at his party."

"You mean the cook-out or whatever it was the night he was killed?"

"Yeah, that's right."

"And why do you think she was the one?"

"Well, she didn't have anything like Randy's Alfa Romeo, but she came in a silver-colored Cadillac, and she had rings on her fingers—diamonds and all."

That would be Erindell Schovall, the lady poet from Deedsville. "Real old"! She may be ten years younger than I am. And there I was naked in Tony's view with my spindle shanks and slight paunch, my gray hair no longer covering my scalp as it once did.

I wondered what Randy's success might have been and

what his game plan was. He and Schovall were reasonably close in age, Schovall somewhat the elder.

"And he showed particular attention to her later in the evening?"

"Yeah. They read poems to each other."

"How do you mean? Off in a corner together?" The picture forming in my mind was becoming interesting.

"Not them," Tony assured me. "No, we all had to go into the living room and listen while she read some old long stuff. And then he read some old long stuff. And the other old woman smoked."

"You don't go for tobacco smoke?"

"Hell, man. It's bad for your health."

"But you use anabolic steroids?" I could not resist the sally.

"Come off it. That's different."

"Well, maybe it is." I chuckled as I got myself dressed.

Once "reclothed and in my right mind," I went into the living room to get those two volumes of poetry, the very fancily bound volumes, which I now thought of as "his" and "hers," the volumes that stood between alabaster bookends on the table under the fancy chandelier.

"See you around," I heard Tony say.

I replied, "Later, alligator!" Well, that was the best I could do.

I had spent all the time I could spare on that afternoon and had not done anything that could be called work. But in terms of enlightenment, the hour had been well worth it.

I took the two books of poetry for future reference and left.

Our Local Bards

HELEN DELAPORTE

I had heard Erindell Schovall read her poetry on more than one occasion. Almost every woman who belonged to a club in Borderville fifteen years ago heard her. We heard her in our own club and then again as a guest at other clubs. But that was when all of us, including Erindell, were younger.

Over the years, she ceased to be a hot item on the Borderville literary club circuit. And the truth of the matter is that we remembered the poet rather than her poetry.

She looked exotic, though we all knew that her mother had been one of the Deedses, for whom the town of Deedsville was named. Erindell got herself up in such a spectacular way!

I suppose she aimed at some inner ideal. In any event, her poetic soul expressed itself in vivid colors, strange hats, and exaggerated jewelry—all of it worn as though put together by chance.

Not a pretty woman at all, she nevertheless took possession of any stage, platform, or lectern where she was allowed to read her poetry. She subdued us, not by her verse, but by her theatrical personality.

It was a strong, masculine voice, and she read with impressive verve. As a result, we remembered her and forgot whatever it was she had said.

I do not regret the number of times I had to listen to her. It was always rather fun. But I never could understand why some of my friends took her so seriously.

Nevertheless, I give her full credit. Coming as she did from Deedsville and continuing to live there, she managed to create quite a commotion wherever she put on her show.

Now, it was catty of me to say that.

But when Henry came home and described his experience in the nude with Tony Braun, I first laughed and then was enchanted by the possible financial link between Erindell Schovall and Randy—and of course a possible link with our mystery.

And, though I had passed up the volumes of Randy's and Erindell's poetry when I first saw them set between those bookends, I was now eager to read every word.

As soon as I got the dinner plates into the dishwasher, I grabbed the two books and ensconced myself in my favorite corner of the living room, convinced that an evening of rare entertainment awaited me.

The volumes were octavo—not very thick— printed on rather heavy paper in order to deceive the reader as to the number of pages within. Both books were printed in Naples, of all places—in 1966. Randy would have been in his late thirties then, his mother already dead. It would have been just about the time he was building his house.

I reflected that Henry had said that Randy's only regular income, so far as he could tell, was an annuity that paid a thousand dollars per month. Of course, he would have had the money from the family home, condemned as it was for the "freeway," and his mother's insurance, and also the proceeds from the policy he had taken out on his friend Pierre. But that would hardly have paid for the present house. Undoubtedly, there had been something left from Mrs. Hartwell's estate, although I imagine her illness had eaten up most of the family fortune.

Randy was egregiously extravagant, and here in my hand was typical evidence of unnecessary outlay incurred about the time the house was being built: a volume of Randy's poems obviously printed at private expense and specially bound in crushed blue morocco, beautifully and tastefully tooled in gold.

The other volume would also have been published privately and was bound in the same manner.

I would have bet any amount that two other volumes bound in the same manner were in Erindell's possession down in Deedsville.

This was clearly a joint venture.

Facing the title page of Randy's volume was his portrait—engraved, no less.

After the title page came a dedication: "To Erindell, my only inspiration."

So much for that. And now for the poetry.

The first poem was entitled *"Tes Yeux."*

> *I look into your eyes and find deep pools*
> *like channels of the sea far down*
> *I run my fingers through your hair and feel*
> *the winds of April rippling there*
> *I taste your lips—your breasts on mine*
> *and we are paradise divine*

I suppose this is actually a poem. It is so designated by the writer and is arranged in lines. It has a kind of rhythm and ends in a couplet. Also, there is no punctuation.

But when I visualize what is said here, I have great difficulty. The problem is that I am acquainted with both

Randy and Erindell, "his only inspiration." The difficulty is that Erindell's eyelids are quite heavy. Her hair, far from waving like the April winds, is frizzy in a haphazard way, although I may have had the misfortune of seeing it only on her bad days.

And Randy, as long as I have known him, has had that freshly scrubbed, neat, choirboy look.

Now I know all about the biology of sexual attraction—pheromones and all that. And it is certainly necessary for the perpetuation of the race that the not-so-handsome individuals of the species have some other power of attraction. But when I visualize Randy Hartwell, breast on breast with Erindell Schovall, tasting her lips while he looked into her eyes and ran his fingers through her hair, I need to giggle.

I turned from Randy's effusion to Erindell's.

The format of the two books is identical: An engraved portrait faces the title page, and there is a dedication: "To R.H. in gratitude." Gratitude for what? Just look at the first poem!

In Araby

Your fingers sought my tangled hair
As we lay breast to breast.
Your lips were pressed oh they were pressed
To mine. Of this I was aware.
But, oh, my soul—my soul, it lay
Within the cavern there behind your lips—
Captive as in an Eastern tale.
I wail, alas, I wail—
Grow cold about my fingertips.

Living as she does in Deedsville, Erindell might understandably wish a transfer to Araby. But that is the least important thing about this poem. The first poem in Erindell's book, this one seems to be an answer to Randy's first poem. They are "breast to breast" again, and he has his fingers in her hair. They are kissing, and somehow her soul has gotten into his mouth. But something seems to be lacking, because she wails. Then she has to grow cold about her *"fingertips"* in order to rhyme with *"lips."*

I couldn't help thinking that this poem, being an answer to the similar one by Randy, said something genuine about their relationship. She calls herself a captive—no doubt a willing one, and yet it is all imaginary—"as in an Eastern tale."

This does not speak of a relationship that could turn into a successful marriage in Deedsville—or in Borderville. I think Erindell knew it, but perhaps it was the best she could get, and she was making the most of it.

Yet Randy seems to have striven manfully to content his beloved—with what he must have hoped would strike her as the desired response. The following poem is an acrostic. Remember those, where the first letter of each line spells a word or name? "Put them all together; they spell MOTHER." That kind of thing.

> *Enchanting forest of desire*
> *riven with torment*
> *I enter*
> *needing passion from your fire*
> *Do not turn your eyes from me*
> *Enchant me*
> *Laden me with frenesie*
> *Love me still or I expire*

Again there is no punctuation, apparently the hallmark of Randy's verse, which we can only attribute to third-rate imitation. The word "frenesie" may be blamed on some pow-

erful wave of inspiration, but "laden me" is merely bad
grammar, no matter how strong the whisper of the muse may
have been. Randy simply needed a word beginning with L.

The poem seems to say that she is a forest on fire. Not
so he. If he is to feel the contagion, the infection comes from
her. To be sure, he says in the last line that he has to have
it. But remember the necessity of "expire" to rhyme with
"fire." That is where the passion lies—necessity.

On the other hand, assuming there is any sincerity on the
part of either rhymester, poor Erindell is the one with the
problem. She says:

> *Tormenter of my wounded soul,*
> *You have turned away.*
> *Gone now for many a day,*
> *Return and make me whole.*

And again:

> *I saw a sunset on the sea.*
> *I willed you standing there with me.*
> *But you were otherwheres,*
> *And you had other cares,*
> *While poor I was left alone.*
> *My heart was cold as granite stone.*

> *Heart of my heart, my soul, my lust,*
> *Come to me, for I call.*
> *Leap o'er the parapet; enter my room.*
> *Come to me, all in all.*

I can't escape the thought that Erindell entertained a real
and burning passion for Randy—probably the more serious because he was her only chance for a fling with a uni-

versal genius. How was a poet with fathomless capacity for
rapture to find a suitable mate in Deedsville, Tennessee?

But Randy! I am sure I looked upon him with a jaundiced
eye. He had talent, modest though it was, which he could
have marshaled to considerable pianistic skill if he had been
willing. But the ego stood between him and musicianship.
And I sensed that the same ego stood between Randy and
any woman.

And what about Erindell? Where had she been since
1966? In Deedsville. And yet Borderville had never thought
of Randy and Erindell in the same breath.

But was it not quite likely that Randy, pressed for cash,
might apply once more to "that real old lady"—as Tony
Braun had called her—apply once more for something to
bail him out?

I thought of Henry James and his story "Washington
Square." Approached again by her lapsed lover, Cather-
ine Sloper had locked the door in his face. Was it not to be
expected that Erindell's heart in like manner would have
hardened, and would she not in like manner have had her
revenge? Perhaps so; perhaps not.

But I found one more of Randy's poems which, as Henry
would say, I wish to introduce into evidence. It is called
"The Keys":

> *You have given me the keys*
> *and suddenly with magic wands*
> *that brush majestically across the strings*
> *my heart responds*
>
> *You have given me the keys*
> *Deep resonances ring*
> *Something deep within that frees*
> *makes me sing*

You have given me the keys
and music in the night
floats on the summer breeze
and everything is right

If I know anything at all, I know who paid for the publication of Randy's poems. I know who paid for the expensive bindings, and I know who gave him his Bösendorfer concert grand.

And Henry says Randy mortgaged the Bösendorfer. Poor Erindell! If he approached her once more for money, I can understand why she might want to kill him.

Another Intruder

HENRY DELAPORTE

Throughout the middle of June, I continued to work at Randy's tangled affairs when I found the time. I always let myself in by the kitchen door for the simple reason that it was the door nearest the street. From the kitchen, I passed through the dining room and living room to reach Randy's bedroom, where I had his papers sorted and stacked on his desk and waterbed.

You no doubt remember that Randy's Bösendorfer was displayed on a platform in the corner of the living room and that the door of the bedroom opened onto that platform.

The platform was low, a bit over a foot in height—just the height for two steps. But that very moderate height, together with the fact that the light from the open bedroom door flooded the highly polished floor of the platform, drew my attention to what seemed a small pile of stuff at the far side of the piano—a pile that had not been there before but had been knocked or pushed from the top of the Bösendorfer. It proved to consist of the Spanish shawl and the remains of the ceramic vase that had been on the piano.

Had someone been in the house? The kitchen door, through which I had entered, had assuredly been locked. I checked the other two entrance doors and found both of them locked. I phoned Mrs. Shankley and was fortunate enough to find Spud at home. He swore that he had neither been in the house nor given his key to anyone else.

My next call was to Tony Braun at the gym. Tony had not been in the house either.

I knew that the maid who did the cleaning for Randy did not have a key, because it had been necessary to leave the one I was using under the doormat for her on the one occasion when she came in to clear up the debris from Randy's final party.

I examined the rest of the house with care but found nothing else had been disturbed. I got on with the intended work until I had to return to the office for an appointment at four.

I concluded that a squirrel had gotten into the house, possibly through the chimney, and knocked vase and shawl to the floor.

But when I told Helen about the incident and suggested my explanation, she would have none of it.

"Squirrel!" she said. "You ninny, someone opened that piano, and the vase and shawl simply slid off onto the floor."

"But why would anyone open the piano?" I asked.

"Looking for our picture," she answered. She puzzled over that for a minute and then said, "Let's measure."

We took a yardstick into our living room. Helen removed assorted music and books from our piano and opened the lid. Ours is a "parlor grand." The longest string is eight feet. Randy's piano is the concert model. The longest string is nine feet.

The real question was whether the interior at the curved end of the piano was wide enough to accommodate the portrait.

"Of course," Helen speculated, "the original picture

would not be in that heavy frame. It is barely possible that it could have been hidden in the Bösendorfer.

"Oh, Henry! Do you suppose they found our picture and took it away?"

Nothing would do but that we must go to the Hartwell house and measure the interior of the nine-foot grand.

From the outside, it did appear to be large enough.

"Oh dear," Helen wailed, *"why* didn't we think to look in there?"

She felt better, however, after we opened the piano and saw that the music rack, which has to be pushed back as far as it will go before the lid can be fully closed, would have made it impossible to hide Louis-Philippe in Randy's piano.

The only damage done was the shattering of a vase that was the work, as we surmised, of Miss Sprote. Which to my notion absolved her of all suspicion.

I was a bit worried by the thought that the house could be entered at will by—well—either some other keyholder or a squirrel.

We returned home to our evening meal at last.

Who Paints What in Borderville

HELEN DELAPORTE

I am glad Harriet did not give me my assignment until it was June.

Episcopalians tend to take a genteel attitude toward the summer, which is very relaxing for an organist. We move the service from the sanctuary to the air-conditioned parish hall and dispense with the choir for three months. And as we have only the piano in the parish hall, my work is suddenly much lighter.

On the other hand, Episcopal social life continues unabated. We picnic, we party, we enjoy our summers, and perhaps because there are relatively few of us in this mountainous area of Southwest Virginia and East Tennessee, we cohere as larger congregations rarely do.

So there were people in the church whom I could ask about the names of Harriet's list.

The first name I asked about was Frederick Woodcott. I asked Melanie Cromby about him one day when I met her grocery shopping at Kroger's.

"Oh, yes," she said, "I know about him. He's the one that paints horses."

I learned that the Singletons have a picture he painted of one of their Tennessee walkers. I went to their house to inspect it. The picture is over the mantel in their den. They have a spotlight on it, and it is meticulously done. The style of the painting is rather like equine pictures of the middle of the last century.

The Singletons retired here from Ohio and have not yet acquired their own comfortable niche in our society. But they are working on it. Keeping horses is part of that effort. I don't know much about horses, but Frederick Woodcott made the Singleton stallion very impressive in that painting.

There you have it: a large painting—in a somewhat antique style. Could this Woodcott not also imitate the style of Peale? But Henry found out that Woodcott had been called to the home office of his company in Chicago for a couple of weeks in March and April. Still, that would have left him two weeks to produce the forgery we found on the walls of the Chamberlain house.

I didn't cross him off the list. I gave him A+ on his skill, A+ on his interest in an earlier style of painting, and at least C- on availability.

The next name for investigation was that of Princess Poulter. I knew her work—had seen it in numerous shows, usually with a ribbon dangling from it. She is a barn painter. That is, you can count on a tumbledown barn in any scene she paints. They are all very good barns. The grass around them is always ragged, and the fences are weatherbeaten.

Upon reflection, I can see that her work is meticulous. But her husband is the treasurer of the Baptist church and I couldn't see her cooperating with Randy Hartwell on anything, let alone stealing a painting from the Ambrose County Historical Society. Nevertheless, I understand that they have two children about ready for college. For her children, a woman will do what she would never do otherwise.

Perhaps she could have persuaded herself that an exact copy of an old painting was a perfectly legitimate commission.

Judith Wexler . . .

She lives across the street from my friend Denise Bradbury. Unfortunately, Denise is not the kind of girl to be nosy about her neighbors. But that circumstance would not have made a great difference, for it seems that Judith Wexler is something of a loner.

She is divorced—without children—from Ernest Wexler, who was an insurance man here a number of years back and left town shortly after the divorce. It was thought that Judith had income of her own, because although she had a job for a few years after the divorce, she gave it up or was fired. After that, she was rather strange and kept to herself.

"I understand she paints," I said to Denise.

"Yes," she replied. "She is very good, too. About five years ago she entered a still life in a juried competition. You may remember it. It was a cut-glass bowl on a window still with the light refracting through it. It was superb. The judges awarded her nothing. It apparently made her angry, and she has never exhibited since."

I did indeed remember the painting—certainly a tour de force. So that was who she was!

"She is definitely peculiar," Denise continued. "I wonder whether she ever got over the divorce.

"She has this awful dog—Weimaraner—keeps it in the backyard. There's a chain-link fence that's pretty high, but the dog gets out now and then. He's been a bone of contention—oops! Well, anyway, there are a few of the neighbors that will not speak to her because of the dog."

After this bit of information, Denise paused before adding: "I feel sorry for her. She is exceptionally talented. She doesn't seem to have any friends. Maybe her painting takes the place of all that. And then when she was passed over in a juried show . . ." Her voice trailed off. "I know I would have been disappointed if I had been in her place. The neighbors think she drinks, but I can't believe it."

I had now gone through each of Harriet's suspects, with the exception of Charlie Gunn and Maybelle Sprote.

I thought once of breezing into Charlie's flower shop and simply asking him if he ever painted in oils. Then I reflected that Charlie knows who I am from my many purchases in his shop; and because of the *Banner-Democrat* story, my name was prominently connected with the mystery of the missing portrait. If he was our culprit, I would be giving my game away by approaching him on any subject related to art. And if he was not our culprit, he would have every right to be offended by my question.

I had a similar problem with Maybelle Sprote. I had met her, and it was quite possible that she would remember. But it is not unusual for people who go in for the more exalted crafts to pursue various other forms of art as well. And then I rather remembered that Maybelle Sprote had a master's degree in fine arts, and that would suggest instruction and discipline—no doubt a thorough course in art history—and if that were the case, we might very well want to move her up to the head of the line of our suspects.

There was no reason to assume that Harriet's list exhausted all possibility. We did not need to be confined to the list of guests at Randy's last—or perhaps "terminal" would be the more expressive word—at his terminal party. Nevertheless, from a distance the people in that gathering were a very strange grouping.

The teenagers. Spud Shankley was by way of being a nephew—actually a great-nephew, and only "half nephew" at that. But to invite him and his girl to a gathering where other guests were much older seemed a bit odd.

The homosexual couple. Holder and Torrence were easily explained if we agreed that Randy himself was gay, but we had by this time found that Randy's sexual preferences were by no means clear.

On the other hand, if we assumed that Randy was attracted both ways, Ted Grigsley, about whom we knew only that he worked for the gas company, may have been at the party as a companion to Randy.

Or perhaps Ted was a companion to Tony Braun, who sunbathed naked by Randy's pool and exchanged rubdowns with my husband!

We thought we knew why Erindell Schovall was present. But why was the Sprote woman there? And yet I could certainly think of Maybelle as lesbian.

The easiest explanation for Randy's guest list is simply that he brought together people whom he could count on to admire him, in which case he probably didn't require any further reason for bringing these people to the same party.

Henry was telling me that the police were still of the opinion that Randy's murder was sexually motivated. With such a curious collection of people at that party, the assumption was logical, especially if we consider the way the body was found—not only nude, but with an exotic dagger in the back. It *did* sound like passion.

But what about the two beds that had been slept in that night? Remember, there had been only one person in each of the beds. As that seemed to rule out the homosexual angle, our suspicion that Randy's murder was connected with the theft of our painting became stronger. Or would there be a connection between the two motives?

Something was about to happen to strengthen our conviction that our painting was the key to the whole mystery. Henry will explain.

The Chewing Gum

HENRY DELAPORTE

In my last account, I explained how Tony Braun and I became good buddies and how I accomplished nothing regarding estate work because of the time I spent with him. On the following day, suffering from an all-over sunburn—well, I never did turn over on my belly but was burned somewhat down my front—I certainly did not intend to repeat my experience.

Grateful that I had not exposed my sitting facilities to the ultraviolet, I determined to go over to the house on Armadale Drive and make up for lost time. Accordingly, I arrived there soon after my Rotary meeting was over.

I turned the key in the lock, opened the door, passed quickly through the kitchen and dining room into the living room. I paused to look through the French doors toward the pool. Tony Braun was nowhere in evidence. I crossed the room, stepped onto the platform on which Randy had mounted his Bösendorfer, and paused, thinking of Helen's theory that the piano had been a gift of Erindell Schovall.

What a set of people!

You must understand that though I am now Episcopalian through marriage, actually I am the son of a Presbyterian minister and grew up in the manse in Shreveport, Louisiana.

That was in another age. I didn't suppose there were people like Randy and Miss Schovall. And here I was in a nest of artistic Bohemians and homosexuals. I had been skinny-dipping and nude sunbathing with a weightlifter less than half my age. How in the world did I ever get involved with such people? I sighed and turned to my intended labors. It is indeed another era.

The door to Randy's bedroom was open— as I had left it. But my first glimpse into the room was a rude shock.

The mattress, if that is what it is called, of Randy's waterbed was lying on the floor—drained of its contents—and the underpinning of the bed was exposed.

If you are familiar with waterbeds, you are no doubt aware that the weight of the water in them is enormous. Unlike other beds, these have no space beneath them. The sides go right down to the floor.

I had never set my mind to consider just how the water mattress was supported across its whole area. I suppose I had thought it might rest on something analogous to flooring nailed to something like sills—perhaps two-by-fours or two-by-sixes.

I now saw that such was not the case. Instead, there were four one-by-eights set on edge in a crisscross pattern.

I immediately realized that someone else had supposed, as I had done, that there was some degree of cavity under the waterbed—a cavity which the intruder perhaps thought was a place to hide a large portrait.

The kitchen door had been locked when I came in. I went back and checked that the French doors and the "front" door were locked. I then examined all windows. The only one that was not fastened shut was the one through which the water from the bed had been siphoned.

I had not reported to the police that we had found the Spanish shawl on the floor with the shards of the vase that had been on the piano. But now the circumstances required that I notify Chief Runnels. I called him, explained both instances of intrusion, and pointed out that the use of a key to enter the house could well be related to the investigation of Randy's murder. He agreed to send Don Cochran out as soon as he returned from lunch.

I put down the phone and went into the kitchen to await Cochran. The refrigerator was humming softly, reminding me that the last time I had looked, there had been some eight or ten cans of Bud in the box.

At that point I realized that I was looking at an empty can of the same variety sitting on the counter by the sink. And next to it was a wad of bright pink chewing gum.

Shortly after this discovery, Cochran arrived. I began by explaining the occurrence involving the broken vase and the shawl. I pointed out that there was a possible explanation of the incident, since squirrels in fact have been known to come down chimneys and romp about inside a house. On the other hand, I observed, squirrels had never been known to empty waterbeds by siphoning the water out the window with a garden hose.

I assured him that in neither incident had there been a break-in. He looked around Randy's bedroom and made a thorough investigation of the whole house. He returned to Randy's bedroom and scratched his head.

I suggested that the intruder had been looking for the Peale portrait. We discussed the possibility a bit. He did not see how anyone would suppose that a painting could be under a waterbed or inside a piano.

I reminded him that the painting was extremely valuable. He agreed that for a prize of such magnitude, a thief would look in the most unlikely places. He agreed also that the intruder was probably involved in Randy's art scam and might even be the murderer.

At this point I related in detail as I remembered it the story Tony Braun had told me about the overheard telephone conversation.

"Why didn't you report that right away?" Cochran wanted to know.

I realized that I should have done so. "I have reported it now," I said in a somewhat shamefaced manner.

I was glad to see that Cochran had brought his fingerprint equipment. He got right to work dusting various surfaces in the bedroom without success.

Then he went over to the Bösendorfer. The pieces of the shattered vase were on the floor where they had fallen. He dusted all surfaces of the shiny black piano, the broken pottery—everything; there were no fingerprints.

I told him about the beer can in the kitchen. It was a forlorn hope. Would an intruder who had been so careful not to leave a trace elsewhere leave a can with his prints on it conspicuously displayed in the room through which anyone familiar with the household would enter?

Cochran dusted anyhow. There were no prints. He put his equipment back in the kit and was turning to leave when I stopped him.

"But the gum," I said.

"The what?"

"The gum. Aren't you going to take it?"

He looked at me in a peculiar way.

The Borderville, Tennessee, police force, you must understand, is no rival of the NYPD. And Detective Cochran was merely the officer assigned, not to arrest disorderly drunks or to ticket speeding drivers, but to trace stolen goods, mostly, and ask questions after one of our locals is knifed in a fight at one of our disreputable bars. He can guess from a shoeprint what the approximate size of the wearer is. He can take depositions. He knows about fingerprints. He knows in what part of town to look for a nest of narcotics dealers. In fact, there are many things he does, and does effectively. But I don't think he had ever had any experience with chewing gum as a clue.

"Look," I said. "Our intruder was clever enough not to leave fingerprints, but he/she was careless about something else.

"How long, do you suppose, does it take the water to drain out of a water mattress?"

"Twenty minutes?" he replied. "Thirty minutes? I don't know. What difference does it make?"

"Only this," I said. "The house is hot, and we are sweating right now. Shut up as it is, the place wouldn't be much cooler at night. Watching the water run out of a mattress cannot be a very interesting pastime.

"Remember that the intruder has a key and therefore can be supposed to know the house quite thoroughly. He knows there is beer in the refrigerator. Why, even I know that, though I have not been in this kitchen so much as one percent as often as the intruder may have been.

"Very well, the process of emptying water from the bed by siphon through the window would hardly deter a thirsty man from coming in here for a drink.

"He opens the can, deposits the gum, and takes his first swig.

"He probably has forgotten or does not know that he can be identified by the DNA in the saliva trapped in that gum—much the same as he can be identified by fingerprints."

Cochran's rather beefy face went through a major change.

"By golly, you're right," he said. "DNA!"

He picked up the gum very, very carefully with his handkerchief.

"You know, that is a great idea," he added. "I would never have thought of it. Thank you. I'll send it to the FBI right away."

So we had a means of identifying the intruder if only we could find the person whose DNA matched the sample contained in the chewing gum.

It all sounded very cut and dried, but there were major difficulties. DNA? How might we extract specimens from the suspect without showing our hand prematurely? We didn't even have the suspect. And if we found our man who matched the DNA in the chewing gum, what could we charge him with? Knocking a vase off a piano? Letting the water out of a waterbed?

Nevertheless, we had a clue.

I Design a Trap

HARRIET GARDNER BUSHROW

It served our burglar right that a wad of chewing gum led to . . . well, I'm not going to tell you just yet what it led to, but it serves that so-and-so right.

If there's anything I can't stand it's a wad of old used-up chewing gum.

People will leave that stuff in ashtrays and, of course, on the sidewalk, where it is specially bad. But I think if somebody left his old gum on my drainboard, I would sure 'nuff be in a snit. So it tickles me to death that the "burglar" came to justice because that nasty old gum was left in Randy Hartwell's kitchen.

And wasn't it clever of Henry Delaporte, the way he saw the gum and realized what it could mean?

I'm not smart like Henry Delaporte and don't have a fine scientific and legal education. When I came along, I was sent to a finishing school because that was considered the best thing for young ladies. I don't complain. Catawba Hall taught me many things that have made my life enjoyable and satisfactory. But when it comes to anything scientific, I just have to take it on somebody else's say-so.

Still, you know, we have all these scientific wonders that have given us television and cellular phones and microwave ovens. Hardly any of us understand them, and yet we have sense enough to be able to use them.

Well, that's the way it was with the DNA in that chewing gum and me. I don't understand it at all, but it sure came in handy.

Now, look at it this way: Henry Delaporte explained that with DNA we could find out who got into Randy Hartwell's house, knocked the vase off of the piano, and let the water out of Randy's bed.

Well, where do we go from there? All we could get out of that would be a trespasser who'd broken a vase, let the water out of a waterbed, and stolen a can of beer. What would that amount to? Twenty-five dollars; fifty dollars? If the vase was anything like the other stuff by that Sprote woman, the loss might not be even that much.

But hold on. The damage was important to us because we thought the burglar was looking for the same thing we were looking for. And if we could find him, we thought it might throw some new light on our mystery.

As I was thinking about that, certain possibilities came to mind. I wrote them down, and here they are:

The burglar was someone who knew that Alberta's portrait of Louis-Philippe had been stolen and was worth a million dollars. Pshaw! Every soul in Southwest Virginia and East Tennessee knew that! They read it in the *Banner-Democrat*.

But not everybody knew that the best place to look for that picture was at Randy's house. We knew it, and the police knew it because Bob Kelsey found that fancy piece of gilt in Spud Shankley's car. And then we also knew Spud had admitted that he helped Randy take the picture back and forth between Randy's place and Alberta's.

The burglar could have been Spud Shankley, but Bob Kelsey asked Spud about it, and Spud absolutely denied he had been in the house when the waterbed was emptied and all that. Well, who else would know to look for the painting at Randy's place? The only other person who could know would be the one who copied the portrait for Randy, because I couldn't imagine that he or Randy would talk about it to anybody else.

The Historical Society got mixed up in this affair only because Alberta left the painting to them in her will. But what about the murder? It would be a pretty big stretch to think that stealing the picture and copying it and so on *wasn't* connected with the murder.

Now, Henry Delaporte learned from Tony Braun that Randy had an argument on the telephone not long before he was killed, with someone who must have been the person who copied the painting for him. That unknown somebody had been promised ten thousand dollars and now wanted more—probably because of the *Banner-Democrat* story.

So, that unknown person was our best candidate (1) to be the one who copied the painting; (2) to be the killer; and (3) to be the "burglar" who left the gum on the kitchen table.

If we were to haul our burglar into court without proof that he was the one who copied the painting or the one who killed Randy, or, better yet, the one who did both, the "burglar" could say: "I was just looking for money," or "I had the key because . . ." And then he could make up something to explain that. He would pay his fine and spend his thirty days in jail. And then he would lie low and never make another move, we would never find out anything more about the mystery, and the killer would never come to justice.

Just think, though: If we could prove that our burglar and the artist who copied Alberta's picture were one and the

same, and if *afterward* we identified the burglar, it would
be more than a case of trespassing and a little bit of damage to the property. I didn't know just what the charges
would be. It would take Henry Delaporte to name them all.
But I would think that fraud and conspiracy would be in
there somewhere, and if it was handled right, murder as
well.

So it looked to me as if we ought to find out for sure
whether the burglar and the forger were the same person.
And that's why I devised my little trap.

Here it is: Take the copy, which we had, out of the frame.
Hide it somewhere in Randy's house—not where it would
be impossible to find, but make it just obvious enough that
it could be discovered. Then wait for the burglar to come
again and find it. If the burglar took the painting away with
him, that would show that he thought it was the real thing
and he was only a burglar and not the murderer and not
even mixed up in Randy's doings. But if he left it behind,
it would show that he knew more about that picture than
he ought to know.

When I called Henry Delaporte and told him about my
scheme, he said he didn't think it would work—said there
wasn't any place to hide a picture as large as Louis's portrait except the places where he and Helen had looked.

"Pshaw!" I said. "Use your imagination. There's bound
to be a way to do it."

All the same, Henry's objection had me stumped.

Then I happened to think of how Dolly Madison got the
portrait of George Washington out of the White House. It
was during the War of 1812, when the British were about
to burn the city. At the very last minute Dolly took her scis-
sors and cut that huge portrait out of the frame. Then she
rolled it up and put it in the wagon with the other things
she was saving.

Now, if you were to cut the portrait of Louis out of—I think they call it a stretcher—you could hide it under a rug, couldn't you?

When I pointed that out to Henry, he had to laugh, and suggested that I should see if Bob Kelsey couldn't come up with a place to hide the forged painting in such a way that it would be found by the "burglar" the next time he/she came on the place. Henry Delaporte was just trying to get out of the job.

So I called Bob Kelsey and told him what I wanted. He was ready and willing and very nice about it, too—nicer than Henry Delaporte, I must say.

Well, that was my first trap. Later on, I schemed up some others. But I won't go into that now.

Mrs. Bushrow's Trap in Operation

ROBERT KELSEY

I've known Mrs. Bushrow a long time. She used to come into the post office like she was the Queen of Sheba. Always nice as you please, greeting everybody and saying something pleasant. Called me by name—would say, "Mr. Kelsey, how have you been since I was in here last?" and "How is that sweet little Leota?"

She was just that way in those days. And she was that way on the telephone, too. I felt that I could almost see her.

She started out the way she used to when she came to buy stamps: "Mr. Kelsey, how have you been since we last spoke?" And she asked about Leota, too. Then she went on to explain that she was in the nursing home getting over her broken hip, which I already knew. Finally she got down to business. She told me what she wanted, which was just the same thing that was in the preceding chapter.

I said I would do it because I didn't know how to say no to her.

Well, the first item was to take the picture out of the frame. That was easy enough. And, do you know, that picture didn't look near as big after that. I actually began to think that there might be some place in Randy's house where I could hide the thing.

I carried it down to Randy's in my van and leaned it against the wall in the living room. I looked around. There were those two big bookcases. You remember, they were let into the wall and appeared to be solidly fastened to it. And they were bigger than the picture I was trying to hide—bigger by a long shot. So I decided to look at them a bit closer.

I was surprised to find that the wood was chestnut. That's the wood that went out of business a hundred years ago when a blight killed all the chestnut trees.

So these bookcases were antiques—probably taken out of old Judge Weathercott's home, the one Randy tore down to build the new house. If that was so, I wondered just how these shelves were fastened into the wall.

They were fitted there in such a way as to be recessed about an inch. If I could figure how to get one of them loose, I could pull it out and put the copy of the king's portrait behind the bookcase and shove the blooming thing back almost to where it was before. It wouldn't be quite the same as the other bookcase, but there wasn't much difference, and I think the idea was to draw the attention to this bookcase so that the person trying to find the picture would look for it there.

That person might wonder why he never noticed that one of these bookshelves was not as far back in the alcove as the other, but maybe he would think he hadn't paid close enough attention the first time around. That would be specially true if he did his looking at night and just with a flashlight, which would be the way I would think he would make the search anyway.

I won't go into the details about how I got that contraption loose from the wall. It's enough to say that I had to take all those books and knicknacks off the shelves. And then I boogered Randy's antique bookcase to a fair-you-well before I got the dad-gummed thing out. But it was a perfect hiding place, and I set the picture right in there before I put the bookcase back.

It was pretty obvious what I had done, the way I nailed it up. But I figured that would just encourage anyone who thought the real picture might be back there behind everything. Besides, when I got the books and doodads back on the shelves, you didn't notice quite so much the place where I had roughed up Randy's fine antique.

You might think our intruder would give up after trying twice without finding what he was looking for. But a million dollars is a pretty good lure, and I agreed with Mrs. Bushrow that our fish would likely snap at it again.

When I finally stood back and looked at my handiwork, I was just like a kid: I could hardly wait to see if our little scheme would really work. Every morning, right after breakfast, I would go down to Randy's and check.

Sure enough, about four days later, the trap sprung. The minute I stepped into that living room, I saw that our burglar had prized that bookcase right out—tipped it over, don't you know—must have used a wrecking bar and did a whale of a lot more damage to the bookcase than I did. All those books and knicknacks were spilled out on the carpet.

Mrs. Bushrow was absolutely right. That sucker had found the picture and laid it out on the floor and stomped on it—and then got a knife out of the kitchen and slashed it from top to bottom.

And that was a shame, because it was a good picture even if it was a fake.

I tell you a fact: It looked like a crazy person had been in that room.

My Second Trap

HARRIET GARDNER BUSHROW

As soon as we found out for sure that whoever was doing all that snooping over at the Hartwell place was the same one who made the copy of the stolen portrait, I went to work to think up another trap. I felt that we just had to get Alberta's painting back and see that it went to the Historical Society as she wished it to.

Poor Alberta! I almost think it didn't bother me so much that the Historical Society was losing out on a million-dollar painting as it did to think that someone would interfere with the last wishes of a dear, sweet soul who wanted to share with the people of Ambrose County something that had been prized in her family for almost two hundred years. She didn't see that picture as something worth dollars and cents. She didn't even see it so much as a work of art. She saw it as a precious heritage that she could give to the coming generations down here on the Virginia-Tennessee border. Heritage means a lot. It means you can hold up your head and be somebody—because you *are* somebody and you know it.

But I didn't intend to get off on that subject.

Now that we knew—well, we just about knew—that the person who painted the copy was the same one who was looking for the original, I thought it was time to find out who that was and turn him or her over to the police.

To think! You can send a wad of chewing gum off to a lab in Maryland where those experts can analyze it and identify the particular DNA that belonged to the person who chewed the gum. And to think it is because of the spit in the gum!

That wasn't a very nice way to say it, but it points to the problem we were going to have identifying the snooper that left the gum in the house. The lab would find the DNA in the spit left in the gum, but we would have to get another specimen of spit from the culprit and match it with what the experts had found in the wad of gum.

Now, how are you going to collect specimens of spit? You can't go around with Dixie cups saying, "George, kindly spit in this cup," and then, "Amy, you spit in this one. See, we've got your name written right on the cup."

People would want to know why we wanted them to spit in our cups, and we would have to say, "Because we think you got into Randy Hartwell's house looking for that stolen picture. And besides, we were wondering if you were the one who killed Randy."

I wasn't just ready for that.

So, how do you collect spit without letting folks know that's what you are doing? That had me stumped for quite a while.

I'm sure you never go very long without receiving requests for funds in the mail, things like "Feed the starving children in South America," "Save the whales," and "Give money for the Heart Fund." All of those appeals come with an enclosed envelope so that your check will be sure to get to the right address.

Now, if we do send that check, what do we do to the enclosed envelope? We lick it. And if the people at the other end were curious about it, they could find out from the envelope what our DNA is.

So I called Helen and told her my idea.

"There are six or seven people that might be the one we are looking for," I pointed out.

"But why do you think they will send the 'enclosed envelope' back to us?" Helen objected. "I nearly always throw those things in the wastebasket."

"Well," I said, "you must think up a cause that they can't resist. Tell them they may have won a prize. Tell them that some remote relative left them an unclaimed fortune."

"But it would come back to my address," she pointed out. "They would know immediately that there was something not kosher about the proposition."

"I didn't say I knew all the details you would have to go into," I replied. "I'm just pointing out that this is a way you can collect specimens of spit with the donor's name attached. Just get to thinking about it, and I am sure you will have it figured out in no time."

With that I hung up, because I knew that Helen would find a much better scheme than I could ever devise.

And, of course, she did.

About Harriet's Second Trap

HELEN DELAPORTE

While I could only admire Harriet's analysis of our situation and applaud her ingenuity in directing us to a scheme for gathering samples of DNA from our various suspects, I was confident that she could have put the plan into operation quite as effectively as I could, and being, as it were, at leisure in the nursing home, she had vastly more time to spend on the project than I had.

But it is ungracious of me to complain. Harriet is not a member of the Ambrose County Historical Society, and her only involvement in our difficulties was that of a friend—on whom, I must add, I have called for help many times. And she has not failed me yet.

It is one thing to have your own idea, to elaborate on it, and to put it into action. It is quite another to be given someone else's idea and to be told, "Here it is. Take it and run."

I was commissioned to send out an appeal of some kind that would elicit the return mailing of an envelope.

Just how many of such envelopes have you returned? Now, I ask you!

I thought quite a while about this problem and wasn't getting anywhere, when on the very next day after Harriet had set it for me, I opened an envelope from the afternoon mail and read: "Your name has been offered in nomination for inclusion in our *Register of Outstanding. . . ."* Never mind what kind of register it was. I'm in several of those things. The publishers make their money by luring people into ordering the finished product for fifty dollars.

I am well aware that the only reason why my name is so often nominated for such a publication is that I have a master's degree from a well-known institution. And I admit that at one time it flattered my ego to think that the name of Helen Delaporte, church organist, would be printed in company with truly deserving musicians who likewise studied at noted institutions. But the glamour went out of it about the third time around.

On the other hand, I was fairly sure that most of our suspects had not taken an advanced degree from a noted institution. Some of them had not graduated from anywhere. It occurred to me, therefore, that some of them at least might be very happy to be invited to appear in a publication the title of which began: *A Roster of the Most Important Names. . . .* You can finish that title in any way you wish.

Yes, there would have to be a letter and a questionnaire, as well as the enclosed stamped envelope. Nothing would be said about paying money now, though it should be suggested that information on publication would appear later.

And of course the replies could not be sent to me or, indeed, to any other person in Borderville. That would be only too obvious. But I have a friend in Washington. The letters could be sent to her. An address in the nation's capital, I thought, would seem all the more authentic. I could send the letters through my friend. She could pass the replies on back to me.

I called the friend, Millie Ainsworth, and explained what

I was up to. She thought it was rather a lark and agreed immediately to cooperate. All that remained was to devise a covering letter and a biographical form to be filled in and to have the letter, biographical form, and two sets of envelopes printed. And then the hardest part would come: waiting for the results.

It took me two days to devise the covering letter and the questionnaire. But I was rather proud of the results, as follows:

BIOGRAPHY INCORPORATED

3128 Avenue M

Washington, District of Columbia

Biography Incorporated is happy to inform you that your name has been selected for inclusion in our projected publication of *A Directory of the Arts in the Appalachian Region*. This long-needed research tool will join our other award-winning compilations: *A Directory of the Arts in the Ohio Valley* and *A Directory of the Arts in the Upper Mississippi*.

Enclosed, you will find our questionnaire, which we are asking you to complete at your earliest convenience, as we cannot proceed to the editing of the volume until all information has been received.

It is readily apparent that the value of any biographical compository lies in its accuracy and completeness. We therefore urge you to complete the questionnaire as quickly and carefully as may be convenient.

Our publications are designed for use by scholars nationwide, but upon publication, a special

price will be determined for sale to persons whose
names are included.

> Cordially yours,
> Charmian S. King, Ph.D.
> Pres., Biography Inc.

I am especially proud of the phrase *"biographical compository,"* which doesn't actually appear in the dictionary
but sounds important, and who would question the grammar or choice of words of Dr. Charmian S. King?

If my letter sounds dishonest, it is little wonder, since
honesty was not its object. Nevertheless, I felt that my de-
ception would go undetected and that it would very much
appeal to the self-esteem of such artistic types as Erindell
Schovall and those local painters recommended to us by
Harriet's friend, the retired art teacher from John Sevier
High.

The questionnaire, which follows, was even more fun to
write.

Name _____

Address _____

Date of birth _____ Place of birth _____

If applicable, name of significant other _____

_____

To which of the following categories does your
work belong?

A. Music ( )   B. Poetry ( )   C. Painting ( )

D. Sculpture ( )   E. Decorative Arts ( )

F. Drama ( )   G. The Dance ( )

In approximately 300 words, describe your activities in the appropriate category/categories.

[I left a large space for this answer.]

Would you permit the use of your name for publicity purposes? _____

Please sign the following release: I hereby grant to Biography Incorporated permission to use the above information exclusively in the publication to be called A Directory of the Arts in the Appalachian Region.

Signed _____ Date _____

When I showed this to my lawyer husband, he said that if any of my victims ever realized the nature of the hoax that was played on them and wished to sue, he would be glad to take their case. He added, however, that if any of my victims engaged some other lawyer, he would unhesitatingly defend me.

Heroic Measures

ROBERT KELSEY

I defied Leota.

When I told her that I was going to lay over nights at Randy's place and see if I couldn't catch that burglar so we could set a few things right, she said, "You'll do no such thing!"

She told me how old I am and that I ought to have better sense. She said I would get myself knocked in the head or maybe worse.

I reminded her that I was a sergeant in the United States Army when she married me, and I figured I could take care of myself. I told her I had that Colt .45 and I would take that with me, but that didn't seem to make her feel any better.

"You'll shoot yourself," she predicted. "How long has it been since that thing has been fired?"

Well, she had something there. It just reminded me that I would have to get some ammunition, which I did.

Leota gave me a really sour look the first night when I went off with my pajamas and a flashlight—and, of course, the automatic.

I used Randy's guest room—naturally, being that the

waterbed didn't have any water in it. I found clean sheets in the linen closet. So that was all right.

I had all the doors locked, but not to keep the burglars out. I had the doors locked because that was what the burglar would expect.

It was the same with the windows—all closed. And though it was hot and awful muggy, an open window would have been a dead giveaway.

I was in bed by ten o'clock. It was a good bed—comfortable and all—but I was so keyed up it was like it was when I would go coon hunting as a boy and sit out in the dark woods and wait to hear when the dogs had treed the critter.

Finally I dozed off, and the next thing I knew the sun was shining in on me through the window.

I jumped up and went all around the house, but there wasn't a thing to make me think the burglar had been there.

Leota didn't speak to me when I came back to the house for breakfast, but the look she gave me said everything.

I spent the next four nights at Randy's house, and still nothing happened. But the following night about one-thirty I woke up suddenly.

Very suddenly!

Was it glass breaking that woke me? As I asked myself, I heard a tinkle as slivers fell. Then I heard the click as the latch was retracted on the front door—well, not quite the *front* door, but the one from the living room to the side yard.

Immediately I realized that someone had broken one of the little windows beside the door, reached in, and turned the bolt.

So!

But the gum chewer and the picture slasher had a key. Why hadn't he used it?

I eased myself off the bed so as to make no noise and got the automatic from the night table where I had put it handy. It was a matter of three or four steps and I was at the bedroom door, which I had left open on purpose.

The moon was almost full; I could make out the larger shapes in the room—and standing a few feet from the fallen bookcase with the books scattered everywhere was a figure examining the wreckage with a flashlight.

My left hand found the light switch beside the door.

"All right," I said, as the lamps in the room came on. "Just drop that flash and put your hands up."

The man I saw was about five feet eight—light wavy hair, glasses, had on a T-shirt and jeans and running shoes. He looked like a hundred other young fellows. But I was pretty sure I'd seen him before. I just didn't know his name.

"Who are you and what are you doing?"

I was right sharp about it.

"And keep in mind that I've got a gun on you."

"I . . ." he began, and sort of mumbled.

"Speak up! What's your name?"

I would say he was somewhere in the neighborhood of thirty. There was a soft look about him. He didn't strike me as the kind that had much experience breaking into houses.

I squinted my left eye and aimed the .45 right at his face.

"What is your name?" I repeated. I didn't sound like I was willing to wait a spell for his answer.

"Ted Grigsley."

Then I remembered where I had seen him. He was the one who worked at the gas company—in accounts. I had complained to him about a bill a few months before.

"You were one of those fellows at Randy's party the night he got killed," I said.

"Oh, God!" Grigsley was beginning to fall apart. "Oh, God! And it's ruined anyway." He commenced to cry.

Here was a pretty scene: me barefooted in my pajamas holding a gun on a poor guy that was about to go into collapse.

"What is ruined?" I asked.

"The portrait." Grigsley said, looking at the wall to my right, where we had propped the slashed and battered copy of the French king's picture.

Right then I knew for certain that this was not the man who left his wad of gum in the kitchen, the one who let the water out of the waterbed, the one who pulled over the bookcase. No, not him! But whether or not he got his information from the newspaper, he knew about Randy's racket with Mrs. Chamberlain's oil painting. And perhaps he knew a whole lot more, too. He might even have killed Randy.

I asked him, "Did you kill Randy Hartwell?"

Then the boy really fell apart.

"No!" he protested.

"What reason do I have to believe that?" I demanded.

"I didn't. I didn't," he kept repeating. "Why do you think I could kill Randy? Randy was so dear and good to me."

The last part of this sentence was lost in sobs. After a few seconds Grigsley swallowed hard and said in a tone of real agony, "He would be alive now, if I . . ."

That was the hell of a place to stop a sentence.

"All right! If you what?" I commanded.

"If I had just come through that door two seconds sooner."

At this point Grigsley turned into an absolute basket case. I didn't need the gun anymore. I took the boy by the

arm and led him to one of Randy's big soft chairs. Grigsley sort of melted into it.

"I think you had better tell me about it," I said. And in
a minute or two, he began.

"I got to know Randy through Billy Ray Holder and
Tommie," he explained.

That was William R. Holder, the loan officer at the bank,
and his boyfriend.

"All of you gay?" I asked.

Grigsby nodded.

"And Randy too?"

"He was ambidextrous."

That wasn't the word he used. I can't think of it just now,
but it means AC/DC.

"He was always so kind. In a place like Borderville, it isn't
easy to be gay. People don't understand. But because
Randy was such an artist. . . ."

There was another sentence cut off in the midst of life.

But I knew what the rest would have been. There were
those old women in Borderville who remembered what a
sweet little boy Randy used to be and couldn't get over the
way he could play the piano and do all the other things.
Then there were some younger ones that caught the idea.
They saw Randy as kind of a blessing sent from God
Almighty to our town. And so, of course, he was an artist,
and everybody knows artists are different. Since any friend
of Randy's was probably an artist, too, they were all what
you might call exceptions.

"Okay." I said. "Let's get on with it. You said Randy
wouldn't have been killed if you had come through 'that
door.' Which door?"

"The door to the bedroom—the one you came out of."

"You had better explain," I told him.

Well, he had been at Randy's party like Spud had said. The party began to break up at eleven because Miss Schovall had to drive all the way to Deedsville. And by eleven-thirty everyone else had left.

Randy had been helping Grigsley decorate his condo. We have quite a number of those in Borderville now. The painters had been there that day. And when Grigsley got home, the windows had been closed since five o'clock. The smell of paint was just too much. The place was not fit to sleep in.

So Grigsley called Randy and asked if he could put up for the night with him.

Grigsley didn't say he was expecting to be accommodated in the waterbed along with Randy, but if that was what he was expecting, he was disappointed.

Anyhow, Grigsley was put into the guest room.

About two o'clock Grigsley didn't quite wake up, but he heard voices that at first blended in with the dream he was having. Then he realized that one of the voices belonged to someone who might very well have been sharing Randy's waterbed. But if that was the case, they were having a falling out.

Randy was saying, "I told you until I'm sick of it: A bargain is a bargain. You'll be paid as soon as I can sell the Peale. Ten thousand and no more."

Of course, that was where Grigsley got the information that Randy was behind the theft of Mrs. Chamberlain's picture that everybody knew about because of the story in the paper.

But to go on with Grigsley's story—

The other voice said, "You didn't tell me you were going to get a million for the Peale."

And Randy said, "I won't get a million. It's worth more

than that, but the way I have to market it, by the time I see any money, I'll be pleased to have seven hundred thousand."

Then the other voice said something that Grigsley didn't catch.

"Ten thousand," Randy said. "We agreed on ten thousand."

The other person said, "You're cheating me. You have been cheating me for years. I painted for you. I've gone to bed for you. I've even gone through divorce for you. And you treat me like dirt."

"Dirt" wasn't the word Grigsley reported, but you get the idea. Considering what I now know about Randy, I would say the individual was right.

Then Randy said, "Well, it will be years before I can sell the Peale—after all the hullabaloo the Delaporte woman made when she discovered the fiddle we were pulling.

"And furthermore, if you hadn't painted such a damned poor copy, I could have moved the Peale right away," he added. "So get out of here and let me go back to bed. You've turned into a third-rate talent and a lush in the bargain."

At this, the second party let out an undescribable sound followed by, "You God-damned bastard! Don't turn your back on me."

This was followed by a cry from Randy and the sound of a fallen body.

Next, there came, "My God! I killed him!"

At this, it seems that Grigsley came out of his stupor, got out of bed, and ran through the door in time to see a shadowy figure disappearing into the dining room. A second later the screen door in the kitchen closed and was followed promptly by the sound of an engine starting up.

"All right," I said, "so why didn't you call nine-one-one?"

Grigsley was blubbering again. "I was crazy about Randy," he said between sobs. "He didn't love me, but he was kind. No one had ever been so good to me."

No doubt Grigsley repaid Randy with adoration, and that must have balanced out the score between them. There's a tit-for-tat in everything, and sooner or later folks pay for what they get.

After Grigsley calmed down a little, I repeated, "Why didn't you call nine-one-one?"

"I stood there," he continued, "just frozen—for a second. I knew I had to do something. There was that dreadful knife still in his back. I couldn't bear it. I knelt down and took the knife out of the wound.

"I suppose I thought it would help. I suppose I thought he was still alive and I was taking the wretched thing out of his heart.

"But he was dead, and I was holding the knife that had killed him."

"So why didn't you call the police?" I prompted.

"But I was holding the knife," he said, as if that was all the explanation needed.

"Why didn't you put it down and call the police?" I demanded again.

"My fingerprints were on it—on the knife that killed Randy. The police would never believe me. You have no idea what they do to gay people."

Undoubtedly, he had something there. Yet *I* believed him, though I don't care for that brotherhood any more than the next fellow does. When I didn't say anything more, he went on.

"Nobody knew I had spent the night here. If I could just get rid of my fingerprints, nobody needed to know. Randy was dead. Not the police or nine-one-one or anybody else could bring him back. And I didn't know who it was that killed him. Why should I call the police?

"I got a hand towel from the bathroom and went all around the house wiping every surface where they might find my prints. It seemed to take forever. Next to the last thing, I wiped the handle of the knife—because there was blood on it.

"Then I got dressed, and after wiping the door knob, I went out the kitchen door and pulled it to behind me. I must have left it partly open because that was how the paper said Charlie Gunn found it the next morning. I got into my car, which was in the carport beside Randy's Alfa Romeo, and got to my condo about a quarter of four."

Now, all of this was very interesting. But while I was satisfied that the boy's story was correct—broken up the way he was—while I believed him, what he was up to just at the moment was attempted burglary.

"So you came looking for the million-dollar picture?" I said.

He didn't answer.

"Have you been looking for it ever since Randy got killed?" I asked.

"No," he answered. "Not until now."

"It took you some time to think about it," I said. "Or did you have to get up your nerve?"

He didn't say anything, which was as good as admitting that he had been too chicken to try it before.

"Well," I said, "I want you to tell me a few more things before we call the police so you can tell them just what you have told me. You don't have to be afraid. If it will make you feel any better, we have a few pieces of evidence that back up your story."

I was thinking of the DNA results due to come in and

the slashed portrait that made us pretty sure the former burglar was the artist who did the copying for Randy. And now with Grigsley's evidence we knew that the painter was the one who killed Randy.

The only trouble was that we didn't know who was the owner of the DNA in the chewing gum.

But here was Grigsley, who had actually seen that person.

"How tall was he?" I demanded.

"Five feet eight—about like me."

"Hair?"

"Dark, I think. Sort of stringy and long. I just saw him duck out through the door."

"Voice? Would you recognize it?"

"I don't know. The door was closed—the whole time."

"More tenor or more bass?" I asked.

He thought about this for a second. "I would say about like mine."

I saw I wasn't going to learn anything more from Grigsley, so I said, "Now I have to call the police."

He objected—wanted to put it off till the next day. But I wouldn't stand for that. He had vital information, and spooked as he was, I figured he was apt to take off unless we attended to this little matter right away.

The police came and took down my information about the break-in. I explained why I believed Grigsley's story. They already knew about the DNA results to come, of course, because it was the police that had sent the wad of gum to the FBI lab. But I had to tell them about Mrs. Bushrow's trap and how the other burglar recognized the fake and ripped it up. Of course, it was right there and the cops could see it for themselves.

I told them I'd answer any other questions in the morning if they needed me. They took Grigsley downtown to

interrogate him and charge him with breaking and entering.

I am sure he told them the same story he had told me.

When all is said and done, I *am* seventy-one years old,
just like Leota said. So I went home. But I didn't get much
rest because Grigsley had described the killer in terms that
didn't point to any one person. I just kept trying to think
who it could be that would fit that description.

Delivery of the Mail

HELEN DELAPORTE

Millie Ainsworth, my friend in Washington who was receiving the replies accepting our offers of inclusion in *A Directory of the Arts in the Appalachian Region,* proved faithful to her task. The only disappointment was the tardiness (from our viewpoint) with which the nominees responded.

The suspects to whom we had sent queries were: Charlie Gunn, our florist; Tommie Torrence, the computer operator; William R. Holder, loan officer at the bank; Ted Grigsley, the clerk at the gas company, whom Bob Kelsey caught breaking into the Hartwell house; Maybelle Sprote, the artistic potter; Erindell Schovall, the poetic lady who seems to have had an affair with Randy and, we suspected, bankrolled him liberally at one time; Frederick Woodcott, local artist who paints meticulous portraits of blooded horses in impeccable nineteenth-century style; Judith Wexler, the recluse whom Luella Mellursh pronounced the most talented artist in the area; and Princess Poulter, also recommended by Luella, who is the wife of the treasurer of the Blue Ridge Avenue Baptist Church.

I had hesitated to include Tony Braun, our hunk who runs a bodybuilding gym over on the Virginia side. How could his specialty be fitted into *A Directory of the Arts in*

the Appalachian Region, or any other region, for that matter? Yet he had been at that party. So, nothing ventured,
nothing gained. I included him in the invitation.

That made ten questionnaires sent out and ten envelopes
to be returned.

As might be expected, certain of our suspects responded
more quickly than others. The first response contained
four envelopes. Millie was so excited that she called me and
reported the return addresses: Schovall (no surprise, certainly), Woodcott, Poulter, and Grigsley. I told Millie to
hold those envelopes until all were in.

A week later, Millie called again and explained that she
now had replies from seven of my people. She reeled off
the names as I checked my list. All were present or accounted for except Braun, Gunn, and Wexler. I told her to
send the envelopes on to me so that the police could forward them to the FBI laboratory. The mysterious Wexler,
having failed to respond to our "offer," seemed somewhat
out of reach, though that made her all the more interesting
to us. Charlie Gunn might well respond later, but there was
no need to hold up the lab work on his account. As for
Tony Braun, what we knew of him seemed to be innocent,
and I could not imagine how he could produce any sort of
painting, let alone a passable copy of Alberta Chamberlain's Peale portrait. Consequently, he was not even on the
list of suspects. If need had arisen, I suppose Henry could
have collected some sweat from Tony the next time they
had one of their sunbathings.

As soon as Millie's big brown envelope arrived, I got the
evidence to Detective Cochran right away. But first I removed the questionnaires—partly from curiosity, but also
because there might be clues in the answers.

Here are some of the things I found:

Erindell Schovall, considering herself first and above all

a poet, having published both in Europe and America (we had missed her domestic publication), nevertheless listed painting as an avocation.

Frederick Woodcott had been keeping his light under a bushel. He reported numerous commissions from horse breeders in Virginia, Tennessee, and Kentucky. He also reported ribbons of various colors awarded to him at competitions throughout the same states. There was no mention, however, of portraits of human beings.

Princess Poulter had painted several portraits.

Ted Grigsley declared himself an actor, with a degree in drama from a small liberal arts college in West Virginia.

William Holder is an unpublished novelist interested in "the inner conflict."

Maybelle Sprote made no mention of painting, although she confirmed the fact of her master's degree in fine arts.

I was quite surprised about Tommie Torrence. He engages in computer-generated art and publishes a journal, no doubt to a very select circulation, devoted to his subject.

These were the replies from seven of our ten suspects. And each reply excited my imagination in some way.

Consider Princess Poulter. How could a woman with a name like that, whose husband is the treasurer of a prominent Baptist church, be connected with the murder of a man like Randy Hartwell? Yet Luella Mellursh had reckoned her among the best painters in our community, and she had actually been commissioned as a portrait artist. She gave the titles of the portraits she had painted, among which was: *Portrait of Grace Armstrong Holding Her Siamese Cat.* It sounds rather saccharine, and I imagined a preponderance of sherbetlike colors. But perhaps Princess could be more somber when the situation required it.

It is a fact that she sings alto in the Blue Ridge Avenue

Choir, and thus fulfills the necessary qualification of a low speaking voice, which Ted Grigsley could have mistaken for masculine. Ted had not seen the murderer except in the shadows, and the person escaped through the dining room to the kitchen door.

Princess has a successful husband who is respected in the community, and I never heard of her having been divorced, as we now knew from Grigsley's evidence the culprit had been. Still, the Poulters have those two daughters to put through college. Money is always a temptation, as I am willing to admit. But beyond the ability to paint acceptable portraits, nothing about Princess Poulter seemed to justify her presence on our list of suspects.

Now, Maybelle Sprote!

If she was trained extensively in art and was in fact a successful forger of paintings, would we expect her to exhibit and otherwise publicize the fact that she paints extremely well? Would she perhaps keep that side of her talent dark? On the other hand, in spite of the outrageous prices she asks for her rather unusual pottery creations, I could not imagine that she sold enough of those things to bring in a great deal of money. Perhaps forgery, after all, was the principal source of her income.

The one time I met her, she impressed me as being rather masculine. I recalled her voice as soft, but one's voice changes in anger. Does it go up, or does it go down? I would think the former, but who knows? She lives in Ambrose Courthouse. The transportation of so large a canvas as Peale's was a problem for Randy, causing him to enlist the assistance of Spud Shankley. If Sprote was the one who had been breaking into the house looking for the picture, how did she expect to get it back to Ambrose Courthouse in that little car of hers? Could she be mistaken for a man? And had she ever been divorced?

Frederick Woodcott, of all our suspects, was perhaps the most adept with a brush. He is tall, is married, and has four children. Although painting is his sideline (he is a broker), the list of commissions he furnished us on his questionnaire suggested to me that he was well enough paid through legitimate avenues that it would be complete folly to engage in something like Randy's art scam. I discarded him from the suspect list.

Nothing about Torrence or Holder suggested that either of them could have produced a painting in oils. There was that compromising photograph that Henry found in Randy's basement. Yet not one item about this pair could be made to correspond to the information Bob Kelsey had received from Ted Grigsley.

But that brings up the subject of Ted Grigsley himself. What about him? If he was such a fine actor, how much could we depend on the story he told Bob? Though we admitted that he was not the painter of the forged portrait, he could have manufactured a story to confirm our suspicions that the forger also killed Randy. This would then divert suspicion from himself and/or others who had no talent in the painting line. Grigsley was certainly looking for the Peale canvas when he broke into Randy's house, but he could have known about the painting accidentally or otherwise, and perhaps he had in fact killed Randy to secure the canvas, only to fail to find it.

On the other hand, it would stretch the imagination to believe that he could produce so emotional a concoction on the spur of the moment.

Three days after I received that large brown envelope from Millie, she forwarded one lone envelope to me. It was the last to be received, and it came from Tony Braun. Yes, Tony considered himself available for inclusion in *A Di-*

rectory of the Arts in the Appalachian Region. He listed himself as an artist's model.

On every score, I had already discarded Tony as a suspect. He did not conform to any of the things we knew or surmised about the killer or the forger. Nevertheless, I gave Tony's envelope to Detective Cochran to be forwarded to the lab.

Something Else for the Stew

HARRIET GARDNER BUSHROW

Although Helen had got eight of those envelopes back from her friend in Washington, it turned out that none of them came from our gum chewer.

It looked at first like we had gone to all that trouble for nothing. But viewed the other way, just two of the envelopes were missing, and that cut the field down to just two people, namely, Charlie Gunn and the Wexler woman. So our suspicion would have to light on them. The next thing was to eliminate one or the other from the running.

Things were beginning to work out very nicely.

Take this Grigsley who broke into Randy's house. Here he was, a witness to the murder, even if he hadn't actually seen it. And yet, what he had heard almost made up for that. It's a pity he didn't mention it sooner, but thank Providence for small favors! What that fellow heard was mighty interesting, even though it didn't settle a number of very important points.

In the first place, everything Grigsley reported could apply about as well to a woman as to a man—that is, if you are willing to allow some unusual sexual preferences to a few of Randy's friends.

Lord have mercy! We never talked about such things in

my day, and now it's on TV, and the preachers and politicians are falling all over themselves saying on the one side that it's just horrible and on the other that it's nothing to get excited about. Well, let them fight it out. I'm glad I'll soon be out of this world and won't have to worry about it.

As to what Grigsley said, let's see which foot the shoe fits—Charlie Gunn's or Judith Wexler's.

Charlie's the one we know most about. He grew up here, and nearly everybody likes him. That means that we have a prejudice in his favor.

Mrs. Wexler is an outsider, and that's against her. She has no close friends, and nobody seems to know much about her. So it's hard to be fair.

I don't pretend that I was on the fence about Charlie Gunn. There never was anybody who was more a gentleman in his manner than Charlie, and he was well spoken and so polite! I never went into his shop to order flowers that Charlie didn't pin a carnation on me or give me a rosebud to take home. Of course I knew I was paying for it in the price of my order, but it felt nice the way he did it. And he was always sympathetic when it was a matter of flowers for a funeral or a memorial.

Now, Charlie had been married. I remember when it happened. The girl was Dorothy somebody. I don't know where Charlie met her, but she was not from here. She was a pretty little thing, and it is too bad that they broke up. People said it was Charlie's mother that caused the trouble, and there's no doubt that Viola Gunn would be a difficult mother-in-law.

But it just might have been Randy who was the cause of that divorce. After all, Luella Mellursh had both Charlie and Randy in her art class, and she said Charlie was just about the only friend Randy had when he was a boy. So it might have been a homosexual thing that broke up the marriage, and that would fit with what that Grigsley man heard just before Randy was murdered.

As for Mrs. Wexler's divorce, when you think of what went on between Randy and that poet woman, you have to consider that there could have been some of the old-fashioned garden variety of hanky-panky between Randy and Wexler. And then, we know for a fact that she paints in oils, but we're not sure about Charlie.

So it could be either one, according to what Grigsley had heard just before Randy was killed. And remember: Neither Wexler nor Charlie Gunn had sent back the envelope to Helen Delaport—the FBI hadn't cleared either of them.

Now, way back when Henry Delaporte found those photographs in Randy's basement, Helen brought them out to show them to me. Not the pornographic ones—she told me about them, but I guess she didn't think they were proper for an old lady to see.

But the photos I did see were interesting enough. You remember what they were like. They were in pairs. I'll call one pair A and B, and the other C and D, and so on.

Photo A was always a straight photograph of a vase of flowers—real flowers, that is. Then B would be the photograph of a painting of the same flowers. Oh, they were not the same exactly, but the flowers in A always showed up in B—maybe in a slightly different place or form. And then there would be objects in B—a deck of cards or maybe a letter, just something decorative—things that didn't appear in A. And don't forget there was that dagger in one of the photos—the dagger that killed Randy—just lying there by the vase.

It stood to reason that the flowers—that is, the real flowers, not the painted ones—that the flowers would have come from Charlie's shop. And the original arrangement would be Charlie's, too.

I still had those photos—in my "Bureau of Investigation." And the more I looked at them, the more I wanted to know what Charlie knew about them. Was he in fact the one who arranged the flowers and painted them too, or did he just arrange the flowers and not know anything about the other photos?

One day I showed the photos—the ones that had been taken of the oil paintings—to Luella Mellursh.

"These are some pictures," I said, "that Mr. Delaporte found among Randy's things. They remind me of water-colors."

"Oh no," she protested. "There is nothing in these pictures that would suggest watercolor."

"Really?" I acted surprised. "I remembered what you said about Charlie Gunn winning prizes with his water-colors, and since he can do such wonderful things with flowers. . . ."

"Oh, Charlie couldn't paint anything like this," she insisted. "These are old, old floral studies. I wonder where Randy found them. Most likely picked them up somewhere in Europe."

I knew better, of course, because I had the photos from which the pictures had been painted. And if there were two pink roses in one of the photos, there would be two pink roses in the painting that was made from the photo, and so on. And the presence of the dagger and other objects that Randy owned ruled out the possibility of the situation being the other way around; the flowers couldn't have been arranged to copy old paintings.

"Look here," Luella pointed out, "around the edge of the painting you can see that it's an old, old canvas on a stretcher." She looked first at one of the pictures, then at another. "No doubt they were painted to be a series. It's odd that they are not in frames."

Now, wasn't it, though! I imagine that by the time they were sold, they *were* in frames—"old, old" frames to go with the "old, old" pictures.

"Flemish, I would say, or Dutch," Luella declared as she gave them back to me.

My hip was getting better and better every day. I was walking quite a bit with my walker, and the rest of the time just scooting my wheelchair wherever I wanted to go. But the real place I wanted to go was Charlie Gunn's flower shop downtown. And I would want it to look as if I was just dropping by casually—as if I had happened to think of something as I was walking down the street. But there's nothing at all casual about an old woman hobbling around with a walker.

So I had to turn the matter over to Helen. She'll tell you what she did and how Charlie reacted.

Photo ID

HELEN DELAPORTE

Mrs. Bushrow gave me my orders, and since her orders always make sense in the long run, I tend to follow them fairly closely and at my first opportunity.

Charles Gunn's shop is on Seventh Street, next door to the law office of the late Angus Redloch, the old lawyer who gave me information about the Drover family when we were trying to solve the murder of Luís García Valera. The shop is narrow, although it runs far back. In consequence there is little display space in the show window. That window, nevertheless, is always a work of art, a spot of color, a surprising instance of beauty on a dull, dusty street of shabby buildings and cracked sidewalks.

I entered the shop through a miniature forest of potted azaleas and hibiscus. Charlie came immediately in answer to the door chimes.

"Mrs. Delaporte," he said brightly. Charlie is perhaps an inch taller than I. "It has been some time since you have dropped in. How have you been?"

I agreed that I had not seen him lately. And how had I been?—well, I had been busy. How was his mother?—and so on.

With this out of the way, he asked, "What can I do for you?"

"Nothing, really," I said as I opened my purse. I took out the photos, wrapped in facial tissue so that he could not see them until I showed them.

"My husband, as you probably know, is the administrator of Randy Hartwell's estate," I continued. As I mentioned Randy's name, I looked into Charlie's eyes. If there was any reaction, it was slight.

"Randy did not leave a will, you know," I added, and waited to see what Charlie would say.

There was a slight pause.

"I know," Charlie said.

"That seems so strange." Again I paused. "There are so many valuable things in the house—things that someone would treasure."

The pauses were part of Harriet's instructions. They made for a very awkward conversation.

"You were a close friend of Randy's, weren't you?"

Harriet had advised me to be impertinently personal, and I was playing the role to the hilt. "Make him nervous," she had said, "and keep your eye on him."

"Yes," Charlie replied, but he did not elaborate.

"And such a dreadful way to die!" I said.

I was invading the man's privacy inexcusably. But it had to be done. Or was it in vain? Even if this interview led to the identity of the killer, would that bring the return of our property? And finding the portrait was my only justification for being concerned with Randy's death in any way.

"How could anyone actually drive a knife into the heart of another human being?" I said. "And such a strange-looking knife! I suppose it was probably lying there on the end table beside the sofa. I am sure you are more familiar with it than I am."

I cannot say that Charlie was indifferent to the things I was saying. He was so entirely in command of himself that I could not attribute his silence to guilt or suspicion or anything of the sort. Nevertheless, I went on.

"And there appeared to be nothing taken from the house."

Here again there was a slight pause.

Then Charlie said, "I hadn't heard."

"Oh, yes," I said and described each of the subsequent forays, in none of which had anything been taken.

"Since there was no will," I observed, "everything goes to the nephew. I can't imagine he will value the sort of things Randy had in his house."

"No," Charlie said, "I have thought about that. Spud and Randy were such opposites. You would never think that they came out of the same family."

Charlie did not exactly relax, but at least he was reacting to my conversation. From Charlie's point of view there were things of Randy's that were merely thrown away on Spud, whereas Charlie would have treasured them. If there had been a will, Randy might at least have left his closest friend the grandfather clock, perhaps—or his books on art. Those things were most appropriately Charlie's, but by law they were Spud's, and Henry was bound to protect Spud's rights.

At this point I unwrapped the photographs.

"Henry came across these," I began, "among Randy's files in the basement. When I saw them, I immediately thought of you. I thought they ought to be yours. Perhaps Randy made them for you."

I showed Charlie the first photograph. It featured tulips prominently. "It's such a beautiful arrangement. As soon as I saw it, I knew you must have done it."

"Yes," he said. "I did this for Randy several years ago. Randy had a thing about the arrangements I did for him. He was very particular about what I could and couldn't use in them. He didn't want them for a dinner or a party or anything like that—just took pictures of them. That was when he was first into photography."

I put the print in Charlie's hand. He looked at it closely and then held it at arm's length, regarding it with obvious pleasure.

"Then there's this one," I said, handing him the second photograph.

It was an arrangement featuring roses in the same way that the first had featured tulips.

"Centifolia," he said.

"I beg your pardon?" I said. In reality, I had not caught the word.

"Centifolia," he repeated. "That's a rose that has one hundred petals—give or take a few dozen. It's a specie rose—hundreds of years old. Modern roses are developed from specie roses. This one has such a lovely pink flush. You wouldn't believe what a time I had getting this for Randy. He was after me about it for almost a year."

Charlie's sudden volubility struck me as the kind of thing I would have to report to Harriet.

"Tell me about Randy and 'centifolia,' " I said.

"It's quite a story," Charlie began. "I was at Randy's one day, and he was showing me a book he had just gotten—a book on Flemish painting, it was—large, very high grade black-and-white reproductions of floral paintings.

" 'Would these roses be white?' he said.

" 'No,' I said, 'this is a pink rose.' Then I explained about centifolia.

" 'Well, get me a dozen, and make me an arrangement something like this one,' he said.

"That was easy to say, but very hard to do.

"You see, centifolia are not grown commercially for their blossoms. They bloom for only a few weeks in the spring. They do not produce long stems, and their petals fall after a day or two. Of course the color is delicate—almost unearthly—and the fragrance is very special. As you can imagine, they don't transport well.

"But Randy just had to have them.

"Finally I found a rose fancier near Rogersville who had several varieties of centifolia. She was glad enough to give the blossoms to me if I would come get them. I went down with the van and got them."

Van!

I tuned out on Charlie's monologue momentarily when I heard that word. We had thought about the van. Here it was—mentioned in connection with a project of Randy's.

I hoped that my face had not betrayed me while I was not listening. I returned almost immediately to what Charlie was saying.

"I didn't even come back to the shop. Randy had the vase he wanted me to use—you see it here," Charlie pointed to the photo.

"Randy thanked me, and I would say he *ought* to thank me. But he didn't offer to pay my expenses. He just said, 'Thanks,' and I went on home. That was how it was with Randy—terribly demanding. But at other times he couldn't do enough for me.

"So he wanted the centifolia for this photo here!" Charlie concluded, handing the two photos back to me.

"Oh, no," I exclaimed. "Don't give them back. I intended for you to have them. That's why I dropped by."

Charlie thanked me and seemed quite pleased.

I then brought out the first of the companion shots showing the paintings made from the flower arrangements. The photos were in the order prescribed by Harriet, the first being the painting with the tulips.

It was clearly based on Charlie's arrangement. There were the same number of tulips. But the tulips in Charlie's arrangement had been Darwins—tulips of the type I have always grown in my own yard. The tulips, however, had been altered in the painting. Instead of the solid colors we expect of tulips, the artist had painted tulips that were of widely variegated hues.

Charlie was clearly surprised by the print I had handed him.

"I can't believe this," he said. "Did Randy paint this? He always went in for the nonobjective stuff. Frankly, it never appealed to me, but Randy always thought of paintings as decoration—something that went with the upholstery and the drapes. He had a wonderful eye for color. But this!"

Charlie was obviously admiring the work.

"Randy kept after me to get him some striped tulips. When tulips were first introduced into Europe, most were striped. About thirty years ago there was an effort to popularize them again, but they did not have much success. When it comes to painting, I guess you can make your flowers any color you want." Charlie shrugged his shoulders. "I never saw this painting," he declared, "but it's based on my arrangement. That's clear." A puzzled look came over his face. "You don't suppose . . ." he began.

"That it is a forgery?" I completed the thought. "Painted to be taken for an old Dutch or Flemish work?"

"Oh, my God!" Charlie exclaimed. He knew that we had discovered that there had been a forgery of the Peale canvas, and he had now made the connection between that forgery and the print in his hand.

"Do you think Randy could have painted this picture?" I asked.

"No, I don't," he responded with great resolution. "Randy was good at all kinds of things, but he was not good at art."

I showed him the fourth photo—the one in which the ornamental dagger was lying beside the vase that held Charlie's recognizable arrangement of centifolia. I held it, however, with my thumb over the dagger.

"The centifolia!" he exclaimed. "Even more difficult to paint than they were to find."

I moved my thumb, revealing the dagger.

"That's it!" he almost shrieked. "That's the knife the *Banner-Democrat* said Randy was killed with. What on earth was Randy mixed up in?"

"That's very much the question," I said. "And more to the point, who was in it with him?"

There was a confusion of thoughts in Charlie's mind at that moment. I could see that he was trying to make sense of it all, when suddenly an alarming thought seemed to take possession of him. He appeared to be horrified.

"I have never seen these pictures before," he insisted. "I admit that the arrangements were mine, but I had nothing to do with the rest of it. I don't want these prints. Take them back." He looked at me as if I had betrayed him, and I suppose that in essence I had. But the fact was that in my own mind I had just proved him innocent.

I gathered up the prints and said, "I'm sorry if I have offended you."

"No offense," he said. "Just take the prints and leave."

As I stepped out of the shop, I was embarrassed about my colloquy with Charlie. I *had* offended him. I was excusing myself on the grounds that it had been necessary to do so. But when a friend dies, we like to think the best of him, and I had planted disappointment—and, apparently, something even more uncomfortable, suspicion.

It remained for me to recount this experience to Harriet, which I did as soon as I could get to the Borderville Nursing Facility. I found Harriet eager and prepared to hear all.

"Now, tell me," she said. She had got herself seated on a sofa in the common room. Her walker stood nearby. I sat beside her and reeled off my information.

"Darling, you have done well," she pronounced. "Let's just look at what we know."

Then we began to lay it out:

First, we were convinced that Charlie Gunn had been no more than innocently involved in Randy's art scams. Moreover, it seemed that at first the art fiddle had not involved the forgery of any specific, recognized painting. It appeared that Randy had been creating, or causing to be created, canvases of a decorative nature that looked old and could be passed off as antique.

If a picture is dark enough and grimy enough, ignorant buyers will accept the painting on the chance—just possibly—that it is a Rembrandt! And if the vendor makes no claim to know the provenance, perhaps there is nothing il legal in the transaction, though beyond question it is a dirty trick.

Between us, Harriet and I settled it in our minds, first, that the phony Flemish flower paintings had been sold through decorators who were outlets for the confidential dispersal of furniture and works of vertu belonging to the financially embarrassed—the same trade that Harriet had deduced from her examination of Randy's crooked books.

Second, it was obvious that Charlie Gunn was innocent of Randy's murder. His dismay when it struck him for the first time that his friend had been engaged in something illegal, or at best shoddy, indicated to both of us that there had been no bad blood between the two.

And that meant in the third place that Charlie's innocence removed him—as we saw it then—from the list of suspects, and left us with Judith Wexler. She corresponded in every detail to the description that we drew from Ted Grigsley's evidence: low voice, divorced, involved in Randy's art scam.

"Darling, we're getting close," Harriet pronounced with conspicuous satisfaction.

"Yes," I said. "We know who did it, but can we prove it in court?"

All the things that we had found were no more than indications. We needed solid proof.

"We'll just have to think of a way," Harriet said with finality.

With that I took my leave. But if I had known what would follow, I would have stayed and protested. I would have shackled Harriet to the sofa. I would have reported her to the police. I would have put her under peace bond.

I should have known what she would do, but I didn't.

Call to Arms

HARRIET GARDNER BUSHROW

Helen's report was like a bugle call to me. It told me it was time to get the old lady activated and energized and going strong.

It was almost five months since I broke my poor old hip. I had gone from the bed to a wheelchair to a walker, and I felt like it was time to start acting on my own.

Fred Middleton, my dear old friend and doctor for many years, had said I could leave the nursing facility in two weeks if I could find somebody to stay with me at home.

Well, I found somebody right away: Mary Lizabeth Sykes—the sweet little woman I helped in the literacy program. I tell you, that girl is just so tickled about being able to read.

You remember, she helped me solve the Music Club mystery.* And when we made a book of that little escapade, of course she was mentioned there. So I gave her a copy when the book came out. She read it all the way through—was just excited to death—it was the first book she had ever read from start to finish.

*The Sensational Music Club Mystery (New York: St. Martin's Press, 1994).

I tell you—as you grow older, the thought will come to you now and then: Have you ever done anything really good for someone? And you just wonder. Well, I did one good thing: I helped Mary Lizabeth. And when I asked her if she would come and live with me, she was just delighted.

I am not a rich woman—never have been. So I really couldn't pay her. But she will get room and board free and can go on with her job at the Cup and Saucer. She will clean the house once a week, and I will pay her for that. She will fix our breakfast and supper, and I'll eat TV dinners out of the microwave at lunch.

But I have wandered way off from the subject. What I started to say is that I was about to leave the nursing home anyhow, and I didn't see why I shouldn't get a preview of how that would be while doing a little detective stuff.

So I called Bob Kelsey and explained what I was going to do. We had quite a little argument. He insisted that what I was suggesting was against his better judgment.

But I pointed out that a great many good things came out of something that was against somebody's better judgment. Columbus came to America, and that was against almost everybody's better judgment.

Besides, I told him, it would be perfectly safe because he would be there if I got into trouble. And if I didn't get into trouble, there would be nothing gained or lost.

I didn't tell him so, but I was going to be horribly disappointed if I didn't get into trouble.

Finally he got so exasperated that there was nothing he could do but agree.

Then I asked him what days and what time of day would be suitable for him. He said that didn't matter since he could accommodate himself to whatever I could work out.

Now, I don't know why I do these things, old as I am, but whenever I get into one of these crazy situations, I get so excited, I just feel like I could do anything in the world. The Bible says: "They shall mount up on wings like the eagle; they shall run and not be weary." Well, that's the way I feel every time I start out on an adventure. A little later, when it gets down to the line and I am doing it, my age catches up with me, and I promise myself I'll never do such a thing again.

But my old heart was just a-pumping, and it was a great feeling when I dialed the Wexler woman.

"You don't know me," I said when she picked up the phone, "but I'm Mrs. L.Q.C. Lamar Bushrow, and I need to talk to you about a certain picture."

At that she slammed down the phone.

That just showed that I was on the right track, because why would she have a conniption about such a simple statement as that if she didn't know exactly what I was talking about?

I dialed her number again, and as soon as she was on the line, I said, "You had better listen, because I have some information you want. I know where that picture is."

Well, she said nothing, but she didn't hang up.

"I need money," I said. "I've had this broken hip, and the expenses have just eaten me up, and I need money— bad."

"What's that got to do with me?" She had a low voice— whiskey voice—like a man's—perhaps the kind of voice that Ted Grigsley was trying to describe when he told about hearing the conversation between Randy and the one that murdered him.

"You know what it's got to do with you. You're the one that painted the copy of that picture Randy Hartwell stole out of Alberta Chamberlain's house. That picture is worth one million dollars, and you are the one who has been trying to find it in Randy's house."

"I have no idea what you are talking about," she snapped. But she still didn't hang up on me.

"Don't act so smart," I said. "You've been going into the Hartwell house right along—made a mess of that waterbed and pulled over that bookcase. You even thought the picture might be in the grand piano, didn't you? Well, let me tell you, the police have your DNA, got it out of the chewing gum you left in the kitchen, only they don't know it's yours. If I should tell them what I know, they'd pull you in mighty quick. And then where would you be? I know where the picture is hidden, and if you act snippy with me, I'll turn it over to the police. Now do you or don't you want to talk to me about where it is?"

Of course, at that time I had not the ghost of an idea where that blessed painting was, but I sounded like I could lay my hand on it any time I chose.

"If you know where the Peale canvas is, why are you telling *me* about it? Why don't you collect it yourself?"

"I won't say any more over the phone," I said. "You have a key to Randy's place. Meet me out there, and I'll show you where the picture is for a one-third share of the money."

Now, wasn't that enough to make her just furious! Randy had done all the planning, but she had done almost all the work to bring off the switch of the pictures. And she had killed him because he wouldn't give her more than a measly ten thousand dollars. Here I had come along without having done anything to earn it, and I was asking one third.

Well, we talked back and forth. She kept saying she didn't have any idea what I was talking about, but the fact that she stayed on the phone said she knew well enough.

I said I would tell her everything if she would meet me at the house the very next day, which was a Thursday.

I told her to park her car down the street and get into the

house without attracting attention. She must get there at
two-thirty sharp, and I would work it out that I would get
there by taxi about ten minutes later—because I didn't
have a key and it wouldn't do for us to be seen there together.

By the time I got through with her, I had convinced her
I had proof that she had been entering that house and that
I was desperate for money.

As for being there the next day at two-thirty, she didn't
say she would and she didn't say she wouldn't. But I felt
sure she would be there. Sixty-six percent of one million
dollars is still a lot of money, and she didn't know where
the picture was. Neither did I, but that's neither here nor
there. She was sure to be at the house when I arrived.

You see, this was my plan: Bob Kelsey would get there
at two-fifteen and hide. I had never been to the house, but
he said he would be out by the swimming pool where he
could get into the house through some French doors as
soon as I needed him.

Mrs. Wexler would get there at two-thirty and find the
kitchen door locked. That way she wouldn't suspect there
was anyone in the place.

And I would come last at two-forty. Poor Bob Kelsey
would have to wait all that while before the excitement
would begin, but we couldn't take the chance that Judith
Wexler might come early enough to see him before he
could get himself hidden away.

There would be a problem about me. I would have to
call a taxi and sneak out of the nursing home, and it was
going to be hard to do that at just the right time.

You see there's a Mrs. Harwood who generally sits at a
desk right by the entrance to the nursing home, and I was
officially an inmate for whom she was responsible. But the
fact is that Mrs. Harwood is sometimes away from her post

as much as fifteen minutes, and if she is not there, visitors just have to wait until she comes back.

But I couldn't rely on her to leave that desk. So I cooked up a scheme with Luella to lure Mrs. Harwood away as soon as my taxi drove up. It turned out that we didn't have to use the scheme because Mrs. Harwood was somewhere else when the moment arrived, but we were ready for her if it had been otherwise.

It was a glorious day. The sun was so bright in my eyes that I could hardly see. But no matter about that. I was out of doors for the first time in months.

Now I'm going to back up just a little and explain something. As you know, you can never count on the taxi to come just at the exact time you want it. And so I had ordered the cab good and early just in case there was a delay. That meant that I would have to ride around a while so as not to get to Randy's house too soon.

But I had that all figured out. I had the taxi man take me through the cemetery. I know that cemetery pretty well. I have so many friends out there. I had the driver go slow, and I would talk about this one and that one as we passed by their plots. I showed the young man where Lamar is buried and where I am going to be. Then he showed me where his brother is buried, but his little boy is buried in the other cemetery with his wife's people. We had just a pleasant visit until it was time to hightail it over to the Hartwell place.

The driver helped me from the cab and got the walker out, too. He wanted to help me to the door. But I assured him that my "niece" would be at the door to help me into the house. He was such a nice man. I smiled and waved to him as he drove away.

I had heard all about Randy's house, but I had never been there. Whoever heard of a house with the kitchen door almost on the street! I didn't see how the estate would ever sell it. But that doesn't matter, because I think it is going back to the bank anyhow.

As a matter of fact my "niece" was not at the door to help me, but I managed without her.

I commenced calling: "Mrs. Wexler! Mrs. Wexler!"

The house was still as death. I made my way through a door to the left. There was the dining room. I hobbled on through to the door at the other end. There was the living room.

Again I called: "Mrs. Wexler! Mrs. Wexler!"

No answer.

Randy's ideas of furniture didn't consider old folks at all. There were two sofas and several chairs upholstered in white—very elegant and expensive-looking, but the seats no more than a foot off the floor and very soft at that. They looked like they would be dandy to loll in. But how in the world was an old gal like me to get herself out of one of these things if I ever sank into it?

Fortunately, I found a sensible chair—a high-backed armchair. The seat was nicely upholstered in kind of a tapestry. I have to hand it to Randy, whatever was wrong about his character, he had a good sense of color.

Well, I sat down in that upholstered chair and found myself right beside the French doors next to the swimming pool, where Bob had said he would be hiding.

I called again: "Mrs. Wexler!"

Then it occurred to me that the woman might have concealed herself somewhere until she could be sure I had not brought anyone else with me. That was smart of her.

So I contented myself with looking around the room. I was curious about that room, because, you see, that sweet Helen Delaporte had described it to me. Well, it was all Helen had said about it.

Over to the right of me was that great long piano on its stage. Nobody but Randy Hartwell would have a piano on a stage in his living room. Oh, the effect is impressive. That piano is just so shiny and black!

And behind it was the screen that Helen had told me about—three huge panels—and Randy had painted it himself!

The whole thing—the black piano and the screen and all—came off very nicely. Much better than I had imagined from Helen's description—splotches of red and orange set off against a kind of background of gold and silver. All I had to do was imagine Randy in tails seated on the piano bench and I got the whole picture of what Randy intended.

Confound that woman! Where was she? "Mrs. Wexler, there is nobody here but me. You can come out," I called.

With that she appeared, coming through a door at the other end of the room.

"All right," she said as she approached. "If you know where that canvas is, tell me where."

"I think we had better talk a bit before we go into that," I said.

"If you are ****ing me, so help me, I'll choke you." She used a word we all know, and I see it in books quite a bit now, and while I use a good many words nowadays that my mother wouldn't allow, the word Judith Wexler used is one that I am *not* going to put in this book.

"We have business to talk about first," I said in a firm way. "Sit down." This was my party, and I was determined to be in charge of it. "Let's talk about money."

Well, that was what we had come there to talk about, wasn't it? So she sat down opposite me in one of those low chairs I was telling about.

"Now we both know," I said, "that a million dollars is just an imaginary amount. It might be the market price, but to sell the painting as stolen goods, as we'd have to do, we'd get a lot less than that.

"Do you have any idea about how to sell a painting valued at a million dollars?" I asked. "You have to keep in mind," I added, "that it is known to be stolen. You can't just send it to the auction house in New York and sell it to the highest bidder."

And do you know, that woman had not had any practical thoughts about what she would do with that picture after she got her hands on it. I suppose those magic words, "a million dollars," had just dazzled her to the point where she couldn't think about anything but getting possession of the object that would fetch such a price.

"Well, now, you see," I assured her, "you're just lucky I'm so broke that I'm willing to let you in on this deal. And of course, crippled up and old as I am, I can't pull this thing off without help. So you're fortunate to have me interested in working something out. I need a young assistant. And after all, you don't know where the painting is."

I could see that my superior attitude was getting to her. I had no doubt that she had thought I was a stupid old biddy with whom she could deal as she pleased, and it irked her that I was taking control in our little discussion. I just went right on and kept my observations flowing.

"I happen to know the names of several dealers Randy worked through," I informed her. "I'd say none of them would dare to sell anything so widely known to have been stolen. But I also venture to say that we could persuade one of those dealers to contact some other party that would be skilled in making sales of a certain kind.

"Of course we would have to pay the middleman a hefty commission, and that would bring down our part of the take. But it can't be helped."

Then, remembering that Randy, on the telephone a day

or two before he was killed, had chalked up our discovery about his fraud to Wexler's failure to produce a copy of the original good enough to fool an expert, I thought I would annoy her a bit more. I said, "Of course, if the copy had been better done, there wouldn't have been any problem. But then, you and I wouldn't have access to Louis's portrait in that case, would we?"

The expression on Judith Wexler's face grew darker as I continued to needle her.

"Had you thought about how you would transport such a big thing?" I asked. "But never mind about that for the present," I continued. "I'm sure we can find somebody to handle that matter for us. The only thing is, he'll want his cut, too."

The woman's face was showing a redness that was more a blush of anger than a blush of embarrassment, and I feel sure she was somewhat liquored up.

"Now, I know you worked with Randy before. There were those flower paintings and so on that he passed off as Old Masters. I was actually able to trace a picture called *Floral with Centifolia*—your work, I'm sure. Yes, I traced it to a dealer in Cincinnati. I imagine Randy told the story that he was handling it for a family in Baltimore—financially distressed, you know—people that had to part with their family heirlooms.

"I don't know what you got out of it, but Randy got thirty thousand."

That was most unkind of me, but if I was to goad this woman to an open admission, I had to use all my ammunition.

"Now, dear, you must realize," I went on, "that we are dealing with a completely different kettle of fish this time. This time it is out-and-out theft. Randy stole that picture, and you were in on it. And what we are about to do is absolutely illegal. So I am taking a big risk. And that is why I have to protect myself.

"I want thirty percent of the take."

I hadn't given her much time to talk. But now that she had the chance, she was at the boiling point.

"Why in hell should I give you thirty percent!" she exploded. "What have you done that gives you a right to thirty percent?"

"Just calm down," I said, "and ask yourself what you have done that gives you any rights. That copy you made of the picture only made our way harder. And you got so mad you even slashed the copy to pieces when you found it behind the bookcase. Your work is lying right over there. You destroyed it. It doesn't figure into the present discussion in any way.

"There is only one reason why you need me—to tell you where the picture is. And there is only one reason why I need you—a physical reason: I am so bunged up that I can't manage the transportation and sale by myself.

"Randy never told you how he unloaded those flower pictures and so on because he had no intention of letting you set up in the art forgery business for yourself. But I have the names and addresses of the dealers he used, and I have no doubt that I can work out a deal through one of them.

"I think I'm being very generous to ask no more than thirty percent. Maybe that won't be even as much as thirty thousand. But it will cover my expenses and leave me a little something more.

"Now, I have no reason to trust you at all. There is no way I can take you to law if you don't live up to your agreement. So, in order to make sure, I have written a little something I want you to sign—just to be certain you don't take the picture and skedaddle."

I opened my purse and took out a folded leaf from my notebook. I read it to her: "I, Judith Wexler, murdered Randol Hartwell by stabbing him with a knife. . . ."

The woman sprang from her chair and glared at me.

"It's a lie!" she screamed.

"Not at all," I said calmly. "This little statement is just my insurance policy. I have absolute proof that you killed Randy. I'm not prepared to tell you what it is, but I have it."

She was beside herself.

She lunged at me, knocking over my chair.

"Help!" I cried.

Her hands closed around my throat.

I tried to call out again, but I could not.

I am very sorry to have to interrupt my story at this point, but things had gone wrong with Bob Kelsey, and you have to know about that before I can continue.

My Mishap

ROBERT KELSEY

It was my fault. It was all my fault, although Mrs. Bushrow didn't blame me and said that it turned out all right, but she came near getting killed. And that would have been my fault for letting her put on such a cockeyed stunt.

This is the way it happened.

It was Wednesday. Leota had our lunch ready just at twelve like she always does. So we were done with that at twelve-thirty, which gave me a full hour before I was to be over at Randy's place.

It so happened that the carrier on our route was sick and his replacement went a different way and delivered our mail while Leota and I were eating.

There in the box was my August Social Security check. It wouldn't take more than ten or fifteen minutes—maybe twenty—if I put that check in the bank right then.

You'll have to admit that it's hard to pass the time when you know something unusual is about to happen—something such as what Mrs. Bushrow was having me do.

I thought: I can go to the bank, deposit the check, and it will be exactly the right time for me to get over to Randy's house and hide there by the pool so as to be handy to the French doors.

I was going west on Division Street at a reasonable speed, and all the lights were green until I got to the light at Johnston, which was red and just turned to green as I came along.

All well and good.

I got into the intersection, when . . . *wham!* A fellow in an old blue Buick slammed into me.

I felt this awful jar and heard the crash. It was like a ton of bricks was on me. I passed out completely.

The next thing I knew, I was in the Life-Saving ambulance. That old siren was honking away and we were really moving.

"Where are we headed?" I wanted to know.

Somebody said, "To Borderville Regional Medical Center."

"Oh Lord!" I said. "Call the police. They must go to 1225 Armadale Drive as fast as possible."

Somebody said, "The police have taken care of it."

Then everything went black again.

When I came to, the second time, the Life-Saving Crew was carrying me into the emergency room at the Medical Center.

"Did you call the police?" I said.

One of the fellows in the white suits said, "They were right there. You were only a block from the Virginia police station when you got hit. It was the police that called us."

I was a little puzzled by this. But before I could figure it out, everything went black again.

I soon woke up, to find an intern wrapping bandages around my head. I had pains like electric current up and down my left arm. On the whole, I felt like hell. But there was something else I was trying to think of. In just a little while I had it.

"Virginia!" I shouted. "He said, 'Virginia'!"

"Take it easy, old boy," the intern said.

"Easy, hell!" I said. "Virginia Police—not the Virginia Police! Call the Tennessee Police!"

Folks that read this will have to keep in mind that Borderville lies across the state line. We are kind of Siamese twins—one city in Virginia and the other in Tennessee. I live on the Tennessee side and Randy's house is on the Tennessee side. The Virginia Police don't go into Tennessee and the Tennessee Police don't go into Virginia. My accident happened on the Virginia side, and it was the Virginia Police that came, not to Randy's house, but to the scene of the crash.

So poor Mrs. Bushrow was alone in that house with the woman that murdered Randy Hartwell.

I yelled at everyone that was anywhere near and told them to call the Tennessee Police.

The intern called to someone in another room to bring him a hypo; he needed to "sedate me."

"Sedate, hell!" I exploded. "A woman is being attacked!"

Then the nurse came in with the hypo, and thank God, it was Alta Mae Foster, who I'd known since she was just a little tyke.

"Why, it's Mr. Kelsey!" she said.

"Never mind that," I said. "Just call the Tennessee Police and tell them there is an intruder in 1225 Armadale Drive. That's Randy Hartwell's place. There is a woman there, and she's being attacked. Tell them that, and tell them to hurry!"

It's funny how everything changed the minute Alta Mae knew who I was. She got right on the phone and did what I told her. Then she came back and said that the police were on their way to the Hartwell house.

I didn't try to explain about Mrs. Bushrow and what we were up to. Those folks at the Medical Center would have known for sure that I was out of my head if I had gone into all that.

I just let the young fellow go on with his bandaging. It turned out also that I had a fracture in my left arm. Then, too, my car was totaled, and while I was knocked out, they had the dickens of a time getting me out from under the steering wheel, and that resulted in scratches and bruises here and there on my ornery old carcass.

Well, anyhow—now you know why I wasn't there when Mrs. Bushrow needed me.

God Sends Me a Raven

HARRIET GARDNER BUSHROW

Do you remember that sweet old story in the Bible about Elijah? When the old fellow was hiding from King Arab out in a cave and the Lord sent the ravens to feed him? I think of that story so many times when it looks like I've got myself into an absolute pickle and then suddenly everything is all right.

No, the police didn't come—well, not just when I needed them most.

You remember that Judith Wexler had jumped up and attacked me, knocking over that beautiful chair I was sitting in, and I screamed, "Help, help!"

Well!

Suddenly there was this crash, and those doors flew open with such force that the glass shattered, and here came this naked man.

I never saw a more beautiful sight in my life—a great big fellow with muscles like an inner tube under high pressure. (I don't think they have them anymore—inner tubes, you know—but that's what those big shoulders reminded me of.)

He just came striding across that floor like a Greek god and picked up Judith Wexler as if she were no more than a sack of groceries.

"What's going on?" he said in a calm voice.

That Wexler woman wasn't calm, though. She was wriggling and shouting and scratching like a cat being held by the scruff of the neck.

I said, "Young man, you saved my life."

"I think I did," he admitted. He was looking at Mrs. Wexler as if he had never seen a woman so wrought up. "Don't I know you?" he asked.

Mrs. Wexler was swearing and a good distance beyond making polite conversation.

"She was trying to kill me. You saw that!" I said. "We've got to get the police. I'm going to bring charges."

At that, the young man—by this time I had realized that he must be Tony Braun, the one Henry Delaporte found sunbathing by Randy's pool that time—the young man reached down with one hand and tilted the chair I was in right back up. The way he did it, you would have thought that I and the chair together weighed no more than a feather.

But while he was doing so, that woman wriggled free and made for the dining-room door.

She would have got away if Tony hadn't tackled her. There he was on top of her, and she was kicking and screaming, when two policemen showed up.

"You're under arrest," one of them said. He had his pistol out and was pointing it at Tony Braun.

Of course, Tony got up and held his hands above his head, the way they always do, although I don't see how they could have imagined he had a concealed weapon.

Mrs. Wexler was loose now and made a beeline for the dining-room door.

"Not him! Not him!" I shouted. "She's the one. Stop her! She's the one that attacked me!"

I never saw anyone as confused as that policeman was. "But, lady, this guy was raping this other lady."

It was most exasperating. Mrs. Wexler was getting away.

"No, no, no!" I said. "Just believe me. I will explain it all. But you've got to catch that woman. She tried to kill me. She was choking me and this nice young man saved my life. You have got to catch her."

The officer was looking at me as if I had lost my mind. Fortunately, the cut-glass beads I was wearing had scratched my neck when the woman was choking me. I was bleeding just a little, and that convinced the patrolmen that I might know what I was talking about—proof that someone had attacked me, don't you see.

The other policeman ran out after Mrs. Wexler. In about three minutes, he came back with her. Then Tony Braun put his clothes on, and the police took us all down to the station.

It was a job getting through all the explanation that had to be made. Finally that nice Don Cochran came in, the officer who is the police detective. He and I had a long conversation. Then he arranged for a patrol car to take me back to the nursing home while he went off to interrogate Judith Wexler.

Discovery

HELEN DELAPORTE

It was almost four o'clock. I was weeding the petunia bed when I heard the phone ring. My inclination was to let it go. So often when I'm busy outdoors and the phone rings, I break my neck rushing into the house only to hear the last ring while I'm still ten feet from that inconsiderate thing.

This time, however, the ringing went on and on. Someone was very insistent, and the most insistent person I know is Harriet Bushrow. I got to the phone before she gave up, and I soon learned why she was so eager to talk to me.

I was horrified that she had undertaken the stunt described in the previous chapter, and yet not entirely surprised, because she has pulled off that kind of thing before.

She took her own danger very lightly, weighing it against the confession she was confident would emerge from the police interrogation of Judith Wexler. But she had been greatly disturbed by the failure of Bob Kelsey to make his appearance at the agreed signal. Harriet had called Leota, who at that time knew no more than Harriet did. The story had cleared up when Bob arrived home by taxi while Leota and Harriet were still on the phone.

Once the combined adventures of Harriet and Bob had been detailed, she got down to the purpose of her call.

"Darling," she said, "I want you and that good-looking husband of yours—after your supper; don't put that off, because men like to have their food served at the regular time—but after supper, the two of you must take a tape measure and maybe a pair of pliers and maybe a screwdriver and go over to Randy's place. Measure the panels in that screen that stands behind his big black piano. And if the panels measure thirty-six inches by sixty-eight, take the screen to pieces very carefully, because you'll find Louis's portrait inside."

Now why hadn't I thought of that?

Because I had seen the screen before—in fact, a good many years before the Peale canvas was stolen. I don't know if Randy had planned the theft of that painting as long ago as that, or if it was just a fortunate coincidence—for him.

You can imagine my excitement when Henry brought the Pontiac to a stop at the Hartwell place.

That living room could have served as a monument to violence. It was the room where the murder had taken place. It was the room where an attempt had been made on Harriet's life. The wreckage of the overturned bookcase remained just where it had fallen. The shattered French doors added a final touch.

But we did not linger over these thoughts.

My heart was racing with anticipation as I approached the screen. It took only a moment to verify the measurements: Each panel indeed measured thirty-six by sixty-eight.

In ten minutes we had dismembered the screen and stripped away Randy's colorful canvas from the central panel to reveal the genuine Peale portrait beneath. What an irony! We had peeled Peale! Do you suppose Randy had had that in mind when he concocted that hiding place?

There was Louis, looking very plebeian with his straw hat and democratic pantaloons. The Ambrose County Historical Society had its legacy at last.

Conclusion

HARRIET GARDNER BUSHROW

The Historical Society mystery was like the twine that I can't bring myself to throw away.

I don't know if people save twine nowadays, but in my time it was almost a sin to waste anything so precious. We saved it. It was good for our character to do so.

Whenever I get a package that is tied with good string, I pick at the knot and pick at it until I can slip the string off the package. Then I put the string in a certain drawer in the kitchen and promise myself that I'll come back to it when I don't have anything else to do, untie the rest of the knots, splice the pieces together, and wind the whole thing up into a neat ball. Thank goodness the day hasn't yet come when I don't have anything better to do.

What I am getting at is that the Historical Society mystery was just all jumbled up like my string collection.

One of the things that made the Society's mystery so knotty was the fact that we were trying to find out two things: the whereabouts of the picture Alberta had put in her will for the Society and the identity of the killer of Randy Hartwell. And then, too, there were so many things we didn't know about Randy's different activities when we first began to work on the case. Perhaps finding out about some of his goings-on did not actually help us solve the mystery, but knowing about them went a long way toward explaining Randy and why he was killed, as well as why he stole the picture in the first place.

So it seems a good idea to bring all the bits and pieces together in a last chapter.

To begin with, we have to admit that Randy had a good many talents in several directions. If he had developed just one of them, he might have turned into something we would all have been proud of. But his strongest talent seemed to be mischief, and he broke the rules whenever he thought he could get away with it.

When that mother of his sent him to Paris, she didn't know that those folks were going to teach her boy how to be a high-class thief. Randy was such a pretty boy, he could just worm his way into the fine apartments of those old homosexual French roués, and that, I am afraid, was his downfall. You see, he liked to be admired.

Then, of course, when he came back, nobody knew a thing about all that, and the old ladies here were so impressed because he had "studied abroad."

Alberta Chamberlain thought she was helping a fine young musician when she had him put on a series of afternoon musical teas in her big house. But right away Randy saw that big picture hanging on the wall by the landing of her stairs and knew it was worth a fortune. He must have made his plans right then, because he somehow got a duplicate of Alberta's house key, and he measured the size of the picture, too.

The way Randy spent money, don't you see, it is no surprise that he was soon hard up. Most folks would have drawn in their horns and lived in a modest way. But not Randy Hartwell.

So Randy went into the business of handling the sale of

the paintings and silver and so on of poor old people who
didn't care to have it known that they were selling off their
family heirlooms. And somewhere along the line Randy
matched up with Judith Wexler.

Now she was a real find! In no time at all she could whip
up a picture that would pass as an Old Master—especially
if the buyer thought he was cheating a seller who was "too
stupid" to know what a treasure he had. Randy was always
a charmer, and he did his stuff and just about took over the
Wexler woman's life. There was her divorce—and then she
turned into a kind of recluse. Add to that the poor girl's de
pendence on Randy—at least partly—for money, and you
have the kind of love-and-hate situation brewing up like a
storm that finally broke in disaster.

And there she was, ready at hand, just waiting until
Randy needed her to paint a copy of Alberta's picture.

So when Alberta got sick and they took her to the hospital because the end was in sight, it was time for Randy to
get to work. Everything was ready. He had it set up so he
could make a photographic slide of the picture. Then Mrs.
Wexler painted the forged portrait. Meanwhile, Randy took
the real picture back to Alberta's house so that when Alberta's cleaning woman looked in to see that everything was
all right, there would be the picture with nothing suspicious
about it.

Years before, Randy had made and painted that screen
that he had in his living room. All he had to do with Alberta's picture was to substitute it for the middle panel and
disguise it by covering it with the canvas he had painted for
his screen. Since the screen had been around for some
time, nobody would suspect what was inside that center
panel.

And then there would be no trouble about sending the
picture off for sale—to New York, or maybe even to

France, in case they wanted a painting of their king as a young man. You see, it would just appear to be a screen that was being sent—and not a valuable one at that.

So Randy had his long-distance transportation all worked out. But he hadn't figured on moving the painting from Alberta's house and back. And that's where Spud Shankley and his old rattletrap station wagon came in.

By the time Alberta died, it looked like everything was going according to Randy's plan. But then something happened that threw everything out of kilter.

Randy thought the Ambrose County Historical Society was just a bunch of hayseeds that wouldn't know anything. They would accept Judith Wexler's copy of the portrait, hang it in some musty old building up at Ambrose Courthouse, and nobody would be the wiser.

Randy had never reckoned that Helen Delaporte would be president of the Historical Society when Alberta died. And what should she do but show what she thought was the painting to Professor Brenthauser, the husband of one of Helen's old DAR friends and an expert on old paintings.

So there it was. Randy had the real portrait on his hands, but Helen was notifying everybody in creation that someone had stolen a portrait of Louis-Philippe by Charles Willson Peale worth one million dollars. You see, that changed everything for Randy. It was out of the question to sell the painting to a museum or to auction it at one of those big places like Christie's or Sotheby's. If Randy got caught— and that looked very possible—he would be sent to jail. The only thing he could do was sit tight—maybe five or six years—and hope all the hullabaloo would blow over.

In the meantime, he was very short on cash: owed the bank—owed everybody. So there was no way he could pacify Judith Wexler when she came demanding a bigger share of the supposed million dollars.

And that's how Randy got himself murdered.

You know, a million dollars sounds like such a lot of money! That Spud Shankley thought it was a lot, and so did Judith Wexler, and so did that poor Ted Grigsley. All three of them came looking for the Peale portrait. And it was from their shenanigans after the fact that we figured "who done it," as they say.

Of course, we didn't have absolute proof about it. Even the DNA evidence wouldn't prove that Mrs. Wexler was the one who killed Randy. It only showed that she was the one who was looking for the picture in Randy's house.

So I had to provoke her to attack me. That didn't prove anything either, but it gave a reason to arrest her, and under interrogation she gave herself away.

The case hasn't come to court yet. Mr. Delaporte tells me Mrs. Wexler's lawyer is likely to plead insanity, and I really believe the girl is a bit off her rocker, to say the least.

I am back in my own house now. Mary Lizabeth is staying with me and gets my breakfast for me every morning. She is spoiling me. She is such a sweet child.

There is one other thing I want to say before this book comes to an end. Some of the ladies of the Gertrude Morrison Suggs Bible Class at First Presbyterian Church thought it was just awful—that young man Tony Braun bursting in through those French doors naked that way.

But I told them that under the circumstances it was the Lord who sent him in there to save my life, and who am I to complain because that boy came to my aid dressed the way the Lord made him?

I must think of something nice to do for Tony.